WESLEY ELLIS

LONE STAR

AND THE RIVER PIRATES

J

JOVE BOOKS, NEW YORK

LONE STAR AND THE RIVER PIRATES

A Jove Book / published by arrangement with
the author

PRINTING HISTORY
Jove edition / July 1991

ISBN: 0-515-10614-3

Jove Books are published by The Berkley Publishing Group,
200 Madison Avenue, New York, New York 10016.
The name "JOVE" and the "J" logo
are trademarks belonging to Jove Publications, Inc.

PRINTED IN THE UNITED STATES OF AMERICA

10 9 8 7 6 5 4 3 2 1

★

Chapter 1

It was late in the evening when the steamboat *Majesta* came round the bend at White Oak, heading upstream, her stacks puffing black smoke. The pilot put the wheel over and edged toward the eastern shore, pulling the whistle cord. The wood stop at Kingsley's was only a half mile ahead.

In a few moments the boat was in slack water, running easily. There was a stout wooden piling at the wood yard, and the pilot swung the boat alongside it expertly, watching the hands at bow and stern wrap their lines around the uprights. The pilot adjusted the speed of the stern wheel so it turned slowly against the current. Then he pulled out a cigar and leaned on the window ledge.

Along the wharf were poles holding iron baskets filled with burning wood as torches for the wood gang. The pilot puffed the cigar, watching the line of men rapidly tossing cut logs from one to the next, piling them on the main deck near the fireboxes. He clicked open the lid on his big silver watch. Fifteen minutes for the onloading and they'd be off. He could hear the mate down below, shouting at them to hurry it up, and he smiled, thinking of Leona. She was waiting for him at St. Louis. He'd be there in another day, and he'd chase her

1

around the hotel room, tearing her clothes off as she yelled and laughed, loving it . . .

He sighed deeply and tossed the half-smoked cigar over the side. The onloading was about finished. There was a gabble of voices from the passengers on the boiler deck—then he heard the shot.

Someone shouted from the dark—and there was another shot!

What the hell? Was some drunk loose? The pilot leaned out of the big window. The wood gang was scattering, running into the woods. He heard the mate bawling orders—then another shot and the voice was stilled.

And suddenly five men with guns came running across the planks, boarding the steamboat! In a few minutes one of them came climbing to the hurricane deck and pointed a revolver at him. The pilot raised his arms. He was alone in the pilothouse.

The intruder was masked. He said, "Come down, you."

The pilot clambered down the ladder to the boiler deck as ordered. The thirty or so passengers were huddled together aft. Two men had gone through them with a seed sack gathering up wallets and jewelry. Two others had taken the captain into his cabin. They were swift and efficient.

The pilot joined the passengers. A few women were crying and some of the men looked ashen. One man lay on the deck. He had evidently been hit or shot; there was blood on his shirtfront. Beyond him a woman was doubled up, with two others tending her.

The pilot heard one of the robbers growl, "We got it, Dutch."

And immediately afterward the five men fled into the night.

The mate and one other man had been killed by gunshots. Two men and a woman had been hurt, and nearly everyone had been robbed. The captain took the pilot aside. "We's a long way from a town, Mr. Harris. Get us moving, if you will. I want to get to St. Louis in a hurry."

The pilot nodded. There was a doctor on board; he saw the man kneeling by the hurt woman. He climbed to the wheelhouse, and in moments the lines were cast off and he moved the boat into the stream. The relief pilot, Mr. Janes, showed up half-dressed. He had been routed out of his cabin and had his money and a watch stolen.

"Goddamn them, Benny! We got to have law on the river! Ever' damn steamboat ought to have guards!"

Harris agreed, though he knew the chances of getting owners to pay for such precautions were probably slight. Owners, being owners, preferred to take in money rather than pay it out.

Mr. Janes was at the wheel when the steamboat nudged into its berth at the St. Louis levee. The captain sent a boy ashore at once to bring an ambulance and the police. In a short while the boat was surrounded by bluecoats and two detectives were questioning the victims.

In due time they got around to the pilot, Ben Harris.

"The five men were masked," Harris said, "and they were in a hurry. So much so that they forgot to rob me when they called me down from the wheelhouse."

"You were lucky," a detective said. "Anything else?"

"Yes. One of them called another by name."

Both detectives' eyes lighted up. "What name?"

"Dutch."

"Dutch!" The policemen looked at each other. "Could that be Dutch Rollins?" They frowned at Harris. "Was he big or small?"

The pilot shrugged. "Big probably—but it was dark and they all wore dark clothes."

Apparently no one else had heard the name. They took Harris to the station house, where he was questioned again; then he signed a paper and they let him go, cautioning him to say nothing to anyone. Especially about the name.

Jessica Starbuck and Ki were staying at the Trenmor Hotel in St. Louis, not far from the waterfront. They were waiting for Jessie's Aunt Lydia. She had wired that she was coming from Natchez, probably on the *Majesta* because she and Captain Barnes were old friends.

The *Majesta* was a Baily-Keller Line boat, and its schedule was posted in the hotel. They walked to the levee the afternoon

3

the boat was to arrive and were surprised to find it surrounded by police. The boat had been robbed by river pirates!

And Aunt Lydia was in the hospital!

They went there at once, and Jessica, being kin, was admitted to the room, to find Lydia sitting up in bed, her left arm and shoulder in bandages.

"Lydia! What happened?"

"I was shot, child. Those damned robbers shot me!"

"Why would anyone shoot you!"

Lydia sighed. "It was a ricochet. I was simply in the wrong place at the right time."

"It's still outrageous! Ki and I ought to look into this."

"You're a dear girl, Jessie. Don't go and get yourself killed on account of me."

"What do the doctors say? Will you be laid up long?"

"Yes, for a while, I'm afraid." Lydia sighed deeply. "I had such plans for us too."

Jessie smiled. "Save the plans. We'll do them all when you're out of here."

★

Chapter 2

Ki was waiting for her downstairs, and they walked out into the late afternoon sun. "She's been shot—from a ricochet—and she'll probably be in bed for weeks. A smashed bullet tore her flesh pretty badly. I talked to the doctor a moment."

Ki nodded. "You probably want to be with her while she recuperates . . . ?"

"Well, I'd like to, but I'd also like to track down the gang that did this. They might have killed her!"

"They did kill two others on that boat."

Jessie tapped her chin. "Let's find out more about it. Why don't we ask the people at Baily-Keller what they know?"

Ki smiled. "Why not?"

The Baily-Keller Line offices were housed in a handsome red brick building on a corner. Inside, a clerk took their names and the message Jessie wrote out, addressed to the president, Johnson Baily.

The clerk escorted them to the third floor. "This's where the important people have their offices." He turned them over to a pale young male secretary, who showed them into a sitting room.

"Please have seats. I'll give your message to Mr. Baily."

The room had a thick navy blue carpet and polished wood furniture, with fresh flowers in a blue-and-white vase. They had barely sat down when the young man was back.

"Mr. Baily will see you now . . ." He led them to a door, rapped on and opened it.

Baily was a tall, spare man with deep lines in his face. He got up from behind a desk and came round to shake with them. "I once met your father, Miss Starbuck. A great man, great."

"Thank you . . ." She introduced Ki.

"Please sit down. What can I do for you?" He went back around the desk.

Jessie said, "We've come about the robbery that took place aboard the *Majesta*."

Baily was surprised. "Why should you be interested in that?"

"Because my aunt was involved. She was one of those shot by the robbers."

"Ahhh. Yes, I know about it. A great pity. They tell me it was a ricochet bullet that hurt her. She is in the hospital, is she not?"

"Yes. We've just come from there."

"Our company will pay her bill . . ." He fiddled with a paperweight. "But you didn't come here to learn that."

"No." Jessie smiled. "Ki and I would like to track down the robbers. What can you tell us about the attacks? I understand your steamboats have been robbed before."

Baily made a face. "You are well informed. Yes, our boats have been robbed before, several times. But this is the first time there have been deaths." He paused. "Our line owns and operates five steamboats. The *Majesta* is the smallest, the others being side-wheelers. Of course we also have a number of smaller craft that do not haul passengers."

Jessie asked, "Were all the robberies done in somewhat the same manner?"

"Yes, they were."

Ki said, "Are any other steamboats being robbed on the river at this time, Mr. Baily?"

Baily hesitated. "I don't really know. As you are aware, there are many different jurisdictions along the river. As you

6

know, the Mississippi touches seven states."

Jessie said, "The passengers were robbed. Was anything else stolen?"

"Yes." Baily sighed. "There was a shipment of cash in the captain's safe. Fifteen thousand dollars was taken."

"How did they know it was there?" Ki asked.

"I don't know. It was not general knowledge, I assure you. It was put there in secret."

"Do you transport cash often, Mr. Baily?"

"Yes, we do. Goods are sent from here to New Orleans and sold, and the money must be transported back here."

"Why not by bank drafts?"

Baily smiled wanly. "My partner, Mr. Keller, was an old-fashioned man who did not entirely trust banks. So for years we sent the money in our safes and never had any problems." He moved the paperweight around. "We will change all that now, of course, locking the barn after the horse is gone."

Ki said, "Mr. Keller is no longer with the company?"

"He died five years ago."

"So, in effect, you own the company?"

"Yes. I am the major shareholder." He smiled at them. "Is there anything else I can tell you?"

Jessica rose. "You have been most helpful, sir. Thank you for seeing us."

The steamboat had been impounded by the police for the next several hours, until all the boat's crew and the passengers had been questioned.

Jessica and Ki called on the boat's captain, Howard Barnes, at his hotel. Barnes had been on the river all his life and had worked for the Baily-Keller Line for seven years.

He was a stocky man, not tall but very vigorous-looking, probably in his early sixties, Jessie thought. His hair was white, his face ruddy, and he greeted them in a most friendly fashion. He was wearing a blue uniform and showed them to chairs. "How can I help you?"

He was alone in the hotel. His wife was in New Orleans, where he kept a home, he told them; she no longer cared to travel up and down the river.

7

Jessie said, "Tell us what you told the police, if you will."

"Are you connected with the police?"

"No, but we are most interested in seeing that the people who robbed your boat are brought to justice."

"So am I!" Barnes shook his head. "I was in my cabin when the five masked men came aboard at the wood yard. They shot my mate when he opposed them. One other man was killed, and a few, including a woman, were hurt." He stopped. "Can I get you folks a drink?"

"No thank you," Jessie said. "Were you able to recognize any of the masked men?"

"No, of course not!"

"I only meant that perhaps you recognized a mannerism or a voice—"

Barnes shook his head.

"You have been on the river so many years and have doubtless met thousands of people . . ."

"Yes, but I never recognized any of them."

Jessie smiled sweetly. "What else happened, Captain?"

"They came to my cabin, took my money and a keepsake—"

"A keepsake?"

"A gold locket my wife gave me many years ago. It has her picture in it and is engraved with my name on the back. They also took my silver watch."

"The company safe was in your cabin?"

Barnes nodded. He seemed surprised they knew about the safe. Jessie explained that they had interviewed Mr. Baily.

"He told us about the money in the safe."

"Ah ha."

"What else can you tell us, sir?"

"Well, the men ran off the boat into the dark. I assume they had horses waiting . . . The wood gang scattered, but the yard owner, Mr. Kingsley, was found tied up in his cabin. He wasn't harmed, and he could tell us nothing about the five."

It was all he knew. He had heard nothing about other boats being robbed. He stated he was going to talk to Mr. Baily about guards . . .

They thanked him and left.

Next they interviewed the two pilots.

Ben Harris had been on duty when the robbery occurred, and he told essentially the same story as had the captain. And he was curious about their connection to the case. Jessie explained that they had talked to Mr. Baily and made it sound as if they were actually working for him.

She was persuasive; Harris opened up as she batted her lashes at him, and he told them his clue.

"The police don't want me t'tell anyone . . ."

"Yes, Mr. Harris?"

"One of the robbers called another Dutch."

"Dutch!"

"Yeh, I think the one called Dutch was the leader."

The other pilot, Mr. Janes, had nothing to add to their stock of information.

The evening newspaper, the *Tatler*, detailed the robbery, including a woodcut of the *Majesta*. The story also mentioned that the police had an important clue. One of the robbers had called another by name.

"So much for police secrecy," Ki said, reading the item. "Someone on the force is making a bit of money on the side."

"Disgusting," Jessie said.

★
Chapter 3

After Jessica Starbuck and her companion had left the office, Johnson Baily sat for a time, staring at the closed door. He had some knowledge of the exploits of the two and it worried him. Damn him! Dutch Rollins had exceeded his instructions and by so doing had harmed Jessica's favorite aunt. Lesser things had caused vast eruptions.

Unless he were very careful, it could in the end prove a fatal mistake.

Dutch was getting too damned independent! And every one of the robberies was making him more so. Of course every one was lining his pockets. A thing he, Baily, could do nothing about. Baily glanced at the clock on the wall. Soon it would be time for him to go meet Dutch. And he would have to curb his anger. Dutch was not supposed to know about the safe in the captain's cabin. Had he run across it by accident? The wallets and jewelry Dutch and his gang collected from passengers were, by their agreement, his to keep.

But not the fifteen thousand dollars in the safe.

He left the company offices early and stopped by a members-only club and had a drink and some idle conversation, then went down to the livery and hired a bay horse.

It occurred to him to take along young Giles Underwood as a bodyguard. The young man was very capable in an altercation—if Dutch should prove difficult. Baily almost went back to the office to get him, then finally decided against it. He was armed with a Colt revolver and was expert in its use, after all.

He rode south from the town.

He had met Dutch several times before at a farm owned by Julius Rann. Rann lived by himself and had no hands working for him at this time of year. He had been mustered out of the regular army some years past and was a man who asked few questions and seldom remembered anything—so long as he received the small stipend each month.

Approaching the farm, Baily cut across weedy fields and came in by a corral and the weathered barn. Dutch was already there, leaning on corral poles. He was an ordinary-looking man with reddish hair and blinking eyes, dressed in dusty clothes and a cap.

Baily never knew whether or not it was an act by Dutch to look innocent—he'd blink away like an old sharecropper. But he wasn't so damned innocent.

Dutch swung around as Baily halted the bay and said, "Howdy, Mr. Baily," just as if they were meeting to talk about buying a horse.

Baily said, "The others on the boat?" He glanced around.

Dutch nodded. "Like you said. Mr. Rann is out plowin' or something." He jerked a thumb over his shoulder.

"Good. Why the hell did you take the money out of the safe?"

Dutch blinked. "The boys run acrost it, that's all. I figgered it'd look funny if we seen the safe and didn't do nothing about it."

Baily leaned on the pommel. Maybe so. "Where is the money?"

Dutch handed over a grubby sack—reluctantly, Baily thought. He looked inside—packed bills. "Is it all here?"

Dutch nodded again. "All there." He watched Baily shove it into his saddlebags. Then Baily swung down.

11

Dutch said, "I'm sorry about them people gettin' shot, JB. They pulled guns on us. They wasn't nothing we could do."

"The woman pulled a gun on you?" His tone was sarcastic.

Dutch growled. "Nobody shot at her. It was a ricochet."

Baily thrust hands deep into his pockets and strode away, turned and came back to stare at the other. "All right. We'll say no more about it. But this is the last job for a month or so. Let's let it all die out. Right now everybody is stomping around yelling about you shooting women. The police are making a big thing of it. They won't admit it was an accident."

Dutch hung his head and made a face, blinking his eyes like an overgrown kid who had just stubbed his toe. "We oney got a few hunnerd in cash from the passengers, JB. We got to take the rest to New Orleans to sell it—and prob'ly oney get twenty percent for it."

"You'll make out, even at twenty percent."

"We got to go all the damn way down the river . . ."

Baily sighed deeply. Dutch whined like that every time they met. Why couldn't the man keep to an agreement without crying about it? Baily went to his horse and climbed aboard, looking down at the other.

"No more till you hear from me, Dutch." He settled himself. "Let the law figure you've quit for good."

Dutch let out his breath and nodded slightly. Baily turned the horse and rode back the way he had come.

Dutch left the barn and went across the fields to the river road and across it, pushing through brush to the riverbank. The boat was tied up there under a clump of trees, with Lyman Yoder smoking a cigar as he sat on the deck, his feet dangling a few inches above the dark water.

He got up as Dutch appeared and jumped aboard. "You see 'im?"

"Yeah, sure. Let's git us on downriver." Dutch untied the line that held the boat in close and pushed off from the bank as Lyman took the tiller.

Alley Trask's head appeared at the companionway. "Where we goin', Dutch?"

"New Orleans."

"Yeah?" Alley's face lighted up. "Well, fry my ass, it's about time!"

"Get some sail on 'er," Dutch ordered. He yelled down the hatch for the others and looked at Lyman. "Keep 'er in the stream. Let's make us some time."

In St. Louis the Baily-Keller case was handed over to Lieutenant Clinton Ware, a veteran of twenty-three years on the force. He was a big, tough-looking man with a craggy face and coal-black hair. He read over the particulars and put them aside. The Baily steamboat had been held up miles from the city, in a place where he had no jurisdiction. His men had looked over the *Majesta* and had made their reports. Dutch Rollins, they agreed, was the main suspect, and Ware had no idea in the world where Dutch might be found. Probably not in St. Louis. He was doubtless holed up somewhere along the long, winding river, swilling booze and spending the passengers' money on floozies.

But as regulations provided, Ware sent information—and their suspicions—to the principal cities along the river, and hoped for the best. It was all he could do.

So when the lovely blond vision with the sea-green eyes and the tall, dark Chinaman came to call on him, he let them in the office only because the woman brightened his drab surroundings, and for no other reason.

"There ain't nothing I can tell you," he said to her when she explained her mission. "We're doin' all we can . . ."

"I'm sure you are, Lieutenant," Jessica said sweetly. "Are the Baily-Keller boats the only ones being hit by robbers?"

Ware shook his head. "I'm not at liberty to discuss the case, Miz Starbuck. It's police business."

"You'll tell us nothing?"

"Nothin', ma'am." Ware fiddled with some pencils. "When the case is finished, you'll read about it in the papers." He watched her as she rose. He sure as hell wished his wife had a pair of tits like those . . .

He heard her say, "Thank you," and then she and the Chinaman were gone.

13

Outside the station Ki said, "He probably had nothing to tell us anyway."

They called on Aunt Lydia again the next morning. But she was not as chipper; the arm was bothering her more than it had been and they were giving her laudanum for the pain. It made her groggy and they did not stay long.

A nurse told them the wound was healing nicely and that often a patient was more uncomfortable on subsequent days than when the wound was fresh. She was getting every care possible, and the doctor visited her twice a day to monitor her progress.

Jessica and Ki agreed their best clue to follow was Dutch Rollins—if they could locate him or his haunts. They went to the local newspaper office and asked to see whoever was in charge of back issues. It turned out to be a young man named Ned Stagg.

They met Stagg at a long counter on the street floor. He appeared in shirtsleeves, with black protector sleeves over his shirt. "You asked about back issues? What in particular?"

Jessie gave him one of her best smiles. "We want to learn about Dutch Rollins, the robber-murderer."

"Ohhhh! I see . . . Are you with the police?"

"No, we're interested citizens and are thinking of doing a piece on him for an eastern periodical." Jessie was wearing a gray-and-black gown with a red-lined cape, as befitted the fashionable city of St. Louis. She leaned forward over the counter so the young man got the full benefit of her low-cut ruffles.

He took a long breath, then beckoned. "Will you come this way, please . . ."

He led them up narrow steps to the second floor and around people working at desks, all of whom turned interested glances on Jessica. Stagg's bailiwick was a large area behind a metal screen. There were endless shelves on which newspapers were stacked.

Stagg consulted a book, then went down one crowded aisle and fingered cards on which dates were printed. "Let's see . . . Dutch Rollins . . . Ah, I think this is it . . ." He

14

pulled out a newspaper and went back to them, unfolding it on a wide table.

"We don't have much on Rollins. He's a small-time crook, you know. But a while back he robbed a hardware store here in St. Louis and set the building on fire to cover the crime." He riffled through the pages. "Here it is . . ." He turned the paper so they could read it.

Elwin Rollins, twenty-five, known as Dutch, was convicted of robbing the Central Hardware Company of fifteen hundred dollars and setting the building on fire. An accountant, working late, had noticed the blaze and sent a man for the fire department; most of the building had been saved. Rollins had gone to jail for two years.

The man who had brought him to justice was Deputy Sheriff Leon Winger.

Deputy Winger was still on duty. He turned out to be an older man, lean and rather dour; he remembered Dutch very well indeed. "What y'all want to know?"

Jessie said, "We suspect he's behind some steamboat robberies. But we don't know where to start looking for him."

"Grogan," Winger said at once.

"Grogan? Is that a person?"

"It's a little burg on the river south o'here. Dutch was born and growed up there and knows ever'body. Still got folks there."

Ki said, "And none of them will tell us a thing."

Winger showed the merest smile on his leathery face. "There's that. But there's good an' bad."

"What do you mean?"

"I mean Dutch has got enemies, even in Grogan. Dutch can't keep 'is hands off other folks' property or their wimmin. When you git to Grogan, you look up Karl Loder—when nobody sees you do it."

"Thanks, Deputy."

"I hope you git 'im. Dutch is a no-good son of a bitch."

They took passage on a small stern-wheeler, owned by an old river man. He made short hauls up and down the river and across it, with passengers and goods. The boat carried farm

15

produce, animals or anything that needed hauling and was of a size to fit on the boat. Of course the boat had a distinctive smell about it. Ki said he would be able to detect it easily a mile away.

The town of Grogan was on the river, but it was primarily a farming community. The weathered town buildings stretched back from the river, and the boat's captain said to Jessica that the town probably comprised eight hundred to a thousand people, though he doubted anyone had ever made a count.

Very few passengers ever got off steamboats, especially to stay, and Jessica and Ki were sudden objects of curiosity.

They stopped in at the first saloon along the street, and Ki asked a bartender where he could find the Rollins family.

The bartender looked at him coldly. "I got no idea, mister."

In the next saloon, the man said, "You sure you got the right place?"

In the general store, the owner did not know any Rollins family.

Jessica went into the millinery store and asked about her cousin, Karl Loder.

"Oh him. He lives about five miles west." The milliner described the house. Jessie bought some ribbon from her and rejoined Ki.

Before dark they hired a horse and buggy from the local livery and drove west along a trace of road to the house. Karl Loder proved to be a heavyset man with the gnarled hands of a farmer. When they mentioned Dutch, his face clouded. He had no use for Dutch Rollins, he said, and Jessie told him they were actively looking for Dutch, to arrest him.

"We think he's robbing steamboats."

"I wouldn't put nothin' past 'im. He been a no-good all his life. And the rest of that Rollins tribe ain't much better."

"Where do they live?"

"Over east and south, got a farm. But Dutch ain't here now."

"Are you sure?"

Loder nodded. "I keep track o'him when he comes thisaway, me and a few others. I going to shoot the sombitch one day."

16

He sighed. "You didn't hear me say that."

Ki smiled. "What have you against him?"

Loder's voice changed. "He raped m'daughter, Elva—then ran off. Now nobody'll have her." His fists curled. "I itchin' to git him in my sights."

Dutch had been born in Grogan, Loder told them, and had been a wild kid, always in trouble. When he was about five his father had been killed in a moonshine ruckus with some hill folks, and a few years after that, Dutch had left home one night.

"He's sly, but he ain't smart," Loder told them. "Not smart enough to stay outa jail. You can't believe nothing he says and he's a back-shooter. He just plain white trash."

Loder did not know where they should start looking for Dutch, but he was along the river somewhere. "He knows folks like hisself in them river towns, crooks and gamblers . . ."

When they were alone, Ki said, "Dutch'll go to a big town to spend his money, won't he?"

"Like New Orleans?"

"I would. It's just as easy to go to New Orleans as it is a little river town where there's nothing."

Jessie sighed deeply. "And it'll be harder to locate him. Maybe he's planning another robbery."

"That's likely."

"Well, what do you say, New Orleans or St. Louis?"

Ki shrugged. "I say St. Louis."

There was only one hotel in Grogan and it had but three rooms to offer. It was a ramshackle building between a blacksmith shop and the Center Saloon. The owner, a grizzled old-timer who spent his time sitting in the sun, complained that he had only one room to let and it had but a single cot. Ki said he would sleep on the floor.

The only restaurant in town was across the street, and when they entered, the place fell silent. People stared at them, and Jessica smiled all round and seated herself at a table with Ki beside her, solemn as an owl.

The food was palatable, beef and potatoes with bitter coffee. When they left, it was dark outside. There was no one else

17

on the wide street. A few horses waited near saloons, but the town was generally quiet. Jessie could hear the faint sounds of a distant piano but little else.

They crossed the rutted street, and as they came into the circle of light near the hotel entrance, a shot shattered the silence!

The bullet slammed into the plank door only inches from Jessie's head. Instantly Ki rushed her through the doorway as a second shot buried itself in the thick plank. Ki kicked the door closed behind them. "Are you all right?"

"Yes . . . I'm fine."

"Poor light for shooting."

She smiled. "So Dutch has friends in town."

Ki let his breath out. "It looks that way, doesn't it?"

★

Chapter 4

When they returned to St. Louis, they went at once to the hospital. Aunt Lydia was much improved. The doctor had pronounced her out of danger, though she would be a long time recovering completely, and she might never have the use of her left arm as it had been.

She was delighted to see Jessie, who brought her flowers and spent an hour with her, till the nurses shooed her out, visiting time being over.

When she and Ki left the hospital, they went to the police station to call on Lieutenant Ware. Perhaps there had been developments . . .

But Ware could not see them. He sent a sergeant to say he was busy and could not be disturbed. The sergeant, Irwin Tyler, said the police had no new information concerning Dutch or the gang. They had not surfaced since the *Majesta* robbery-murder, and it was assumed that Dutch was off somewhere spending the loot.

"Maybe Memphis or New Orleans, one of them towns."

"Do you have a photograph of him?" Jessie asked.

Tyler smiled. "Yes. There's a jail picture they took of him a few years ago."

Jessie touched his arm. "We would love to have a copy of it, Sergeant."

"I'll see what I can do. That picture oughta be circulated. Trouble is, the lieutenant don't think so."

"Why in the world not?"

Tyler let his breath out. "He's a man got a lot of personal problems." He shook his head. "But there's one thing about Dutch . . ."

"What?"

"He's a slimy crook and a killer—but there got to be somebody behind him with brains. He ain't smart enough to stay outa jail by hisself. I think he's doing somebody's dirty work."

Jessie nodded. Karl Loder had said the same thing. "That's a very interesting idea, Sergeant. You figure someone has hired Dutch to rob steamboats?"

Tyler nodded. "Of course it's just a guess . . ."

"Have you discussed it with Lieutenant Ware?"

Tyler made a face. "He ain't interested in my ideas."

They returned to the Trenmor Hotel, and that evening over supper Ki said, "If Dutch is arrested—according to Sergeant Tyler—the brains behind Dutch will only get another man to take his place, won't he?"

"Yes, unless Dutch talks to the law and implicates him. And I think it's certain that if Dutch is caught, he'll protect no one."

"Which means the brains knows that and will do away with Dutch if the possibility arises?"

"Maybe . . ."

They pulled in to the bank each night and tied up under the trees. There were floating logs in the river, and if a big log slammed into their little boat, it could crush it like an eggshell. None of them was a good swimmer, so Dutch did not want to take the chance.

When they reached Natchez, they stopped for two days, drinking and celebrating with a variety of saloon girls before they went on to New Orleans.

Dutch's favorite hangout in New Orleans was a coffee-house-saloon-brothel called the Spotted Cat. The guarded front door was reached by means of an alley off a side street. Patrons had to know where it was; it had no advertising sign.

Dutch and the others always had money when they went there, and so they were always well received and entertained. They went to the Cat the night they arrived in New Orleans; the middle of the week and the place was sparsely occupied. Lyman, a cardplayer, quickly got into a game. The others talked and joked with the girls, one of whom Dutch soon took upstairs.

Lyman considered himself a card manipulator. Every day he spent time with the pasteboards; he prided himself, in a game, on knowing where every card in the deck was at any time . . . when he was dealing. The cards had kept him in beans many a time when other forms of endeavor, including his pistol, had not.

He sat in with three strangers; they introduced themselves as Jack, Ricky and Todd. Ricky was wearing fancy clothes, near white with an elaborate embroidered vest and silk cravat. He was obviously a gambler.

Lyman looked at Ricky's hands, long pale fingers and lacquered nails, and Ricky measured him and smiled when he saw Lyman deal. Todd and Jack were ordinary creatures.

They played poker quietly with drinks at their elbows and chips stacked before them, dealing, betting and raking in without fuss. Todd, who said he was a businessman, tended to express himself with oaths when he lost, which was frequently, but Jack said little, frowning at his cards.

In the first half hour of play, Lyman felt that someone was nicking the edges. He called for a new deck, but the nicking continued. Who was doing it? Lyman was certain that neither Jack nor Todd had the experience, and probably neither had even noticed it. The most likely candidate was Ricky. If he had noticed the nicking, he should have called for a new deck, and he had not.

Lyman watched Ricky. When it was Ricky's turn to deal, he took off a heavy silver ring and laid it on the table, saying it got in his way.

Lyman eyed the ring. It had a flat, bright surface instead of a stone. As Ricky dealt the cards, his eyes watched the ring

21

and Lyman sighed deeply. Surely this was one of the oldest tricks in the profession, and it annoyed him that Ricky should consider him such a clod.

He said, "Put the ring in your pocket, Ricky, and deal the cards over." He tossed his into the center of the table.

There was an instant silence. Ricky stared at him and his face flushed. "Are you accusin' me of something?"

Lyman said evenly, "Your ring reflects the cards."

Jack and Todd frowned at the silver ring.

But Ricky's hands moved with lightning speed. One hand shot forward and a derringer suddenly appeared in the other. Lyman clawed for his gun, yanked the hammer back—but Ricky fired twice, directly into Lyman's chest.

Lyman's gun clattered away and he slumped to the floor, knocking over his chair.

Ricky scooped up the ring. "He accused me of cheatin'!"

The room had fallen silent. Then, in a moment, everyone was talking at once. A big man appeared at the table. Ricky was reloading the derringer, and the big man's hand closed over it. "You did the shooting, sir?"

"He accused me—"

"You three, pick up your goods and come with me." He pointed to the body, and two bartenders moved in quickly and hauled it away.

The big man ushered the three across the room and into a hallway. He opened a door and they went inside. "Wait here, please . . ." He left them.

The big man had taken Ricky's derringer. Todd said, "Did you hafta shoot 'im?"

"He accused me of—"

Todd pushed Ricky against the wall. "And I'm accusing you too. Let's have the money you won."

★

Chapter 5

Everyone in the club, upstairs and down, had heard the shots, and the owner, Harry Mills, sitting at his desk, leaned back as the big man entered.

"Gambler shot a man over cards. Ricky—you remember him?"

Mills nodded. "Is the other one dead?"

"Yes. He's a friend of Dutch. Name of Lyman."

"Damn. All right, Carlo. Get the gambler outa here—you know what to tell 'im. The body's out back?"

"Yes, in the alley."

Mills grunted. "Fine. I'll talk to Dutch and we'll fix it." He got up as Carlo left the room. The big man would warn the shooter to keep his mouth shut. The shooting never happened. Mills sent a man to find Dutch and bring him to the office.

When he arrived, Harry broke the news. Lyman was dead. His luck had turned bad. Nothing anyone could do.

Dutch said, "Shit!"

"We don't want the law—"

"Hell no!" Dutch said. "Who shot 'im?"

"A gambler. I got him outa here. Forget that. You got to take care of Lyman—all right? He's in a buckboard in the alley. Can you handle it from here?"

Dutch sighed. "Yeah. I got three other boys with me. Where's the best place to plant 'im?"

"Across the river. I'll send Carlo with you to the ferry. Ask him about that."

Dutch went to the door and glanced back. "Thanks, Harry." He went out. One hell of a celebration. Lyman had been a good man . . .

They had wrapped the body in a tattered blanket and put two shovels beside it. Emory and Cy had backed a mule into the shafts; Carlo was waiting, and when Dutch climbed onto the seat, Carlo drove out of the alley and turned north. The ferry was about a mile away, he told them.

Jessica and Ki quickly learned that the main competition to the Baily-Keller Line was the Scully firm, Elliot Scully, president. His line owned seven steamboats, all side-wheelers . . . floating palaces.

Another visit to see Sergeant Tyler told them the Scully boats had not been robbed. "They got guards on board," Tyler said.

Over supper Ki asked, "Is it possible that the Scully people are behind the crimes?"

"Why—to eliminate the competition?"

"Would it be the first time?"

Jessie shook her golden head. "No, but is it likely? The Scully company is obviously very successful. They don't need to resort to underhanded tactics. If things go on as they are, the Baily-Keller Line may fall apart all by itself."

"I suppose so . . ."

But they decided to call on Elliot Scully the next day. When they arrived at his offices, however, they were told that Mr. Scully was away, out of the state, and not expected back in the near future.

In the meantime, Mr. Whiting was at the helm.

John Whiting was an older man who looked, Jessie thought, much like a bookkeeper—and possibly he was. However, he looked comfortable in his job and greeted them with old world courtesy, "How can I help you?"

Jessica said, "We're looking into the robberies suffered by the Baily-Keller Line. We are told your company has had no such losses."

Whiting smiled. "That is true." He seated himself opposite them and twined his fingers in his lap. "We have thought it curious that the bandits have struck only the Baily-Keller boats . . ."

"Have you taken steps?"

"Yes. We employ armed guards on each of our boats, and that arrangement has been made public. Perhaps it has saved us trouble—it's impossible to say."

Ki asked, "Has your business increased because of the Baily Line problems?"

"Yes, a little bit."

"Not substantially?"

Whiting shrugged slightly. "What Baily has lost is spread out among all the carriers of course. We are only one."

Jessie said, "Is Mr. Scully retiring from the firm?"

Whiting smiled. "I am not privy to Mr. Scully's plans. At present he is on a well-deserved and extended vacation with his wife and several friends. I am told he had planned the trip for several years."

Jessie rose, thanking him for his time. She smiled as he kissed her hand gallantly, and they went out.

After planting Lyman in the fertile soil of Louisiana, Dutch, Alley Trask, Cy Carew and Emory Boles took passage north on the tiny stern-wheeler *Macon*, bound for St. Louis. They were four of twelve passengers in all. Most were men, drummers on their way to their territories, with bulging valises and sample cases.

They were generally loud and outgoing; they all knew each other and the crew and spent the hours gambling with dice and cards, shouting and moaning . . .

Dutch and the others kept to themselves and got off the boat at a little burg called Simcoe. Dutch knew the area well. Simcoe was not on the river, but back a mile or two from it. They would have to hike into town.

There was a wood yard not far away, and he proposed they

25

wait there for a steamboat and replenish their depleted funds.

There was a short pier and an embankment where boats tied up, their owners in the town. It could hardly be a better arrangement, Dutch said.

They walked into the town and had supper there, and late in the evening, they walked to the wood yard. Two men were playing cards in a shack. Dutch and the others tied them both up at pistol point. Then they waited for the first steamboat.

Two hours later a northbound boat nudged into the berth, its bells clanging. The boat's crew tied off and the wood gang came ashore. Dutch and his men brandished pistols and the wood gang fled.

Alley Trask and Cy ran across the gangplank and herded the crew aft. Dutch and Emory went through the passengers with grain sacks, collecting cash, jewelry, watches and anything else that took their fancy.

Only one incident disturbed the smooth operation. A young man objected to their taking a gold stickpin and foolishly drew a pistol. Emory shot him twice in the belly amid screams and curses.

Then the four ran across the gangplank and into the dark woods. They returned to the Simcoe waterfront without pursuit.

The area was deserted. Emory cut the lines of a black-hulled yawl; they piled aboard and shoved off. Alley took the tiller, and Dutch ordered, "Git some sail on 'er!"

They drifted into the stream, and as the wind filled the sail the little boat swung south, heeling over as she sped along.

★

Chapter 6

News of the steamboat robbery that had occurred near Simcoe was on the wires within hours. Another passenger had been killed.

Johnson Baily read the accounts in his office and found himself trembling. What the hell had he let loose! The method used was exactly the same as that used on the Baily boats. Dutch. It had to be Dutch!

He dropped the papers onto the desk and went to the window, staring out into the gray sky. What was he going to do about Dutch? The man could not be controlled; he was a criminal through and through. There was no sense thinking of him in rational terms. He would have to be dealt with as a criminal.

He would have to be killed. It was the only way.

But that presented a very difficult problem. How to do it? He would probably have to employ someone as criminal as Dutch. And if he did, would he also then have to do away with the second man?

The safest way would be to do it himself.

He took a long breath. Did he have what it took to shoot

a man down in cold blood? He thought about pointing a gun at Dutch's middle and pulling the trigger—and he found himself with damp cheeks and forehead. It was easy to give the orders—not so easy to carry them out.

He had told no one in the world what he was doing. Actually Dutch was the only person who knew anything at all—Well, old Elliot Scully was part of it, but he had never discussed details with Elliot, and now Elliot was in Europe thousands of miles away on a prolonged vacation. He could forget Elliot . . . for the time being.

Who could he talk to about his problem?

No one, with the kind of answers he needed, came to mind. He did not travel in circles likely to know such things as murder. And how touchy to ask, "Can you put me onto someone who would kill a man for me?"

Baily shook his head. How could he do that!

He had learned about Dutch quite by accident, and he heard about Hap Stoker the same way. He was having lunch with a businessman friend, listening to the other tell about his troubles hiring warehousemen and long-distance overland haulers.

"They steal you blind, Johnny, if you don't hire men to watch them."

"Like Pinkertons?"

"Yes, but, well, you can get men cheaper. I hired Hap Stoker. He came well recommended. He's a sort of broker. He gets the men together to act as guards."

"You hire him and he hires the men. Is that it?"

"Exactly. I tell him the problem and he gives me a price. When we agree, I leave it all to him. And his guards are a rough bunch . . ."

"Is that all he does, guard work?"

"No, I guess he'd tackle anything he could find men to handle."

Baily sipped his coffee, studying the other. "Tell me more about this Stoker."

"He's a big brute, but smart. He told me he came from New England. Only been in these parts a short time. Why? D'you think you might use him on your steamboats?"

"Certainly I might. Next time you see him, ask him to come and see me."

"I will."

Baily thought a good deal of what he would say to Stoker when they met. Murder being a serious matter, it would be well to work into it by easy stages. Stoker might have a mind-set against it, or religious objections. One never knew. He would hire Stoker to guard one of his steamboats.

And if there was a God in heaven, Dutch would pick that particular boat to rob and Stoker would kill him.

Of course that kind of thinking was too good to be true. And guarding the boats would put his plans off, but he could manage that—if it all led to the right conclusion. An enormous lot of damage had been done already, and it would probably cause but a ripple among the stockholders if he put up one or two boats for sale when he got a rumor going that Baily-Keller was failing, going out of business. Most of them must be expecting that now.

All those things were manageable in due time. But Dutch was not.

Hap Stoker showed up five days later and was shown to Baily's office. As the friend had said, Stoker was a big one. He had thick shoulders and a shock of reddish hair. His hands were twice the size of Baily's, and though Baily was not a small man by any measuring stick, Stoker looked down at him when they faced each other.

Stoker's handshake was gentle and his voice was soft. He nodded when Baily said, "Thanks for coming. Please sit down . . ."

Baily discussed guarding the steamboat *Majesta*, asking for Stoker's input. He had a dozen men, Stoker told him, who were afraid of nothing and experienced at guarding whatever. He suggested dressing the guards as passengers. They would shoot to kill any robber who came across the gangplank.

Stoker was so receptive that Baily ventured further. He mentioned Dutch Rollins.

"I've heard of him," Stoker said. "A cheap crook."

"We are certain he's the one who robbed our steamboats.

29

I'm going to put a bounty on his head. Five hundred dollars, dead or alive."

Stoker smiled. "I'd like to collect that . . ."

"I wish you would," Baily said.

The steamboat robbery near Simcoe was in all the newspapers, and the item caught Jessie and Ki's attention. Ki said, "It was pulled off in exactly the same manner, and a man was killed."

"Ummm. But not a Baily steamboat."

"No. Maybe Dutch and his gang needed money."

Jessica frowned. "But they got fifteen thousand dollars from the *Majesta* robbery! Not to mention all the passengers' cash and jewelry. Did they spend all that so soon?"

Ki rubbed his jaw. "That's right. But if they didn't need the money, why rob the boat?"

"Was it someone copying them?"

"That's possible, of course." Ki made a face. "Why don't we call on the boat captain when he arrives?"

The boat was the *Alcorn*, and the captain's name was Perry Brisse. He was a youngish man with thick side whiskers, and when they showed him the prison picture of Dutch, he pointed to it at once. "That's the man who robbed us!"

"Tell us about it," Jessie urged.

"He had three men with him—"

"Three? On the other robberies he had four."

Brisse shook his head. "I'm positive. There were only three. Ask any of the others. They pushed the crew aft, and two of them relieved the passengers of valuables and cash and one shot Mr. Nestor. He died before we could get him to Simcoe and a doctor."

The last glimpse Captain Brisse had seen of the robbers, they were running into the woods. Not much to go on. His opinion was that they would go downstream.

"It's the easiest, quickest path," Brisse said. "They can use almost any boat. If they went across the river, of course, they could go anywhere by horseback—if they had horses. But if they once got in a boat, I'd say they'd stay in it."

"I think he's right," Ki said when they left him. "Everyone

30

tells us Dutch is not smart enough to tie his own shoes. How far ahead does he plan?"

"And what happened to one of his men?"

Ki shook his head. "Maybe he got religion. I say, if he's not smart, then Dutch went downriver. It's the easiest path, as the captain said. Get in a boat and let the river take you."

Jessie smiled. "Why don't we do the same thing."

"Go to New Orleans?"

"Why not? And we have a friend there . . . on the police force."

"That's right!"

It was a long journey in a small boat to New Orleans. But they had a seed sack full of loot to sell, and Dutch was convinced the best fences in the country were in the river town . . . and the best of all was old Isaac Kupper, the German.

On a previous trip, Dutch had left the swag from other robberies with Isaac and accepted a round sum. Isaac was as honest as a man could expect.

When Dutch showed up so soon after, with another sack, the old German was surprised. "You been busy, Dutch."

"All's I do is hold out a sack and they throws the things in. What I gonna do, Isaac?"

The old man laughed. "Bring the sack here. Lay it on the table, Dutch. Let's see what you got f'me."

Dutch shook the glittering pile onto the wooden tabletop. Isaac began to pick the watches out of it, putting them aside. Dutch scratched a match and puffed a cigar, watching. The old man quickly made piles of rings and bracelets, chains and necklaces. "Some of this here ain't worth shit."

Dutch sighed. "You say that ever' time I bring you stuff."

"Because it's true. Lookit this!" Isaac held up a gaudy ring. "Worth fifty cents maybe—to the right hooker."

Dutch took the ring. "It looks real . . ."

"Pish. You got no eye for the real thing. Lookit this one. What would you say?" Isaac held up a stickpin.

Dutch squinted at it. "Another fifty cents?"

"It's a goddamn diamond!" Isaac rolled his eyes. "Two hunnerd dollars in the right market."

Dutch shook his head. "Never mind the lessons. What you give me for the lot?"

Isaac got out a pad and did some figuring, moving the piles he had made one at a time, wetting the pencil, complaining. He would have to file off names and dates, inscriptions, melt silver, hammer gold, pry out gems and put them in other settings . . . a lot of work . . .

But when they settled on a price, he paid Dutch in cash. They had a drink together, and Dutch went back to the cheap river-side hotel and split up the money. They had enough to keep them in tall cotton for a while. And when it was gone they'd go back upriver. There was plenty where that came from.

The Crescent City was a bustling place, a city of vast energy for work or play. Jessie and Ki arrived in the middle of a fine, crisp morning. When the steamboat tied up, Ki hired a strapping boy to carry their things to a hack; then they drove into town and put up at the Dorance Hotel.

At lunch Jessie said, "If you were Dutch Rollins, what would you do if you came here?"

Ki laughed. "We don't know who he knows."

"Well, there's one thing we do know . . ."

"What he looks like?"

"Yes, that too, but I mean the jewelry and other things he stole from passengers. Won't he try to sell them?"

"I should think so. Of course they'll have inscriptions and names on them, so they can be traced. He'd have to sell them to someone who can obliterate them or melt them down. They're evidence."

Jessie smiled. "And evidence leads us right to Denis Foucaud."

"I'll be glad to see the sergeant again."

"I sent him a note this morning."

Denis Foucaud was a police officer they had worked with on a previous investigation for a dear friend of Jessie's father. Denis had proved to be a charming and clever man, and Jessie had many fond remembrances of him and was eager to see him once more.

He came to the hotel as they were finishing lunch, embracing Jessie and shaking hands with Ki, every bit as glad to see them as they were to see him.

"Jessica, you are even more beautiful than the last time I saw you!"

She laughed. "And you are just as flattering."

He said gravely, "I never flatter."

Ki led them to a quiet corner, and they sat, heads together as Foucaud asked, "What brings you to New Orleans?"

"Robbery and murder," Jessica said.

"Your daily fare, Sergeant," Ki added.

Foucaud smiled. "Lieutenant, please. I've been promoted since I saw you."

Jessie clapped her hands. "Congratulations!"

He made a little bow. "So tell me about this robbery/murder. What's it about?"

"You probably know about it already." Jessie filled him in about the steamboat crimes. Foucaud knew about Dutch Rollins—the sheets had come over his desk recently.

"Do you think he may be here in New Orleans?"

"It's quite possible," Ki said. "We think he may have come here to fence the passengers' valuables."

Foucaud nodded. "And it's also possible he may have come here to sell the entire lot to someone bound for Europe. The things could be put aboard a steamer and be out of our reach in hours."

"I hope not," Jessie said.

"Of course we have lists of persons suspected of fencing stolen articles. Do you have a list of the missing items?"

Jessica shook her head. "Unfortunately Lieutenant Ware in St. Louis would tell us nothing. He's in charge of the case there."

"I see. Well, I will officially request the information by wire. We should have it directly."

Denis Foucaud was dark, with a small mustache and square shoulders. His hair was graying at the temples, giving him a very distinguished look. He took out a pencil, and they composed the wire to Lieutenant Ware. He would send it off at once. "I hope this man, Ware, made a list of the items. If not," Denis shrugged, "there is little we can do."

• • •

While they waited for a reply to the wire, Foucaud took Jessica off to see the city. He hired a carriage, and they drove to Jackson Square in the French Quarter, where he had been born and grown up.

They toured the fascinating antiques shops along Royal Street and the old French Market near the river, where they stopped for dinner.

"How did you get involved in this case?" Denis asked over wine.

"Because of my dear Aunt Lydia. She was a passenger on the *Majesta*, a steamboat robbed by Dutch and his men. A ricochet wounded her seriously, and Ki and I vowed to track down the men who did it."

"Ahh, I see."

She took out the photograph of Dutch. "This is the man we're looking for. Taken a few years ago in prison."

He studied it. "Not an impressive type, is he?"

She smiled. "I have never heard him spoken of in complimentary terms."

He chuckled. "May I have this copied and circulated?"

"I wish you would."

He tucked the photo into an inside pocket. "It will be done tomorrow."

★

Chapter 7

Jessica and Foucaud went from the restaurant to his apartment and sat on a shaded balcony with a bottle of cognac. He had never married, he told her. "A policeman's life is not one that many women wish to share. It can be dangerous and there are at times long hours—many drawbacks to a home life."

She smiled. "But policemen do marry. I know this for a fact."

He squeezed her hand. "Then perhaps I have never found the right girl . . . one like you."

"Do you think I could make a wife for you?"

He gazed at her, then shook his head slowly. "No, I suppose not. But it is a most enjoyable dream. You must let me have that."

Foucaud had a large tiled tub in the house, easily large enough for the two of them. He carried Jessie in and undressed her, kissing her as his nimble fingers unhooked her gown and laid it aside.

Then, naked, she slid into the steaming water as he deftly removed his clothes and tossed them away. He looked down at her for a brief moment, his manhood erect, then stepped into the water and slid his arms about her from behind, pushing

35

against her firm, round buttocks. Jessie grasped his arms and held him tightly, leaning her head back.

"It's been a long time," he said softly.

She rubbed herself against him sinuously. "Let's not talk about time . . ."

He caught up a bar of soap and began to massage her with it. "Very well. Let's talk about soapsuds . . ."

Jessie laughed and turned in his arms, taking the soap and scrubbing his matted chest. His hands were free to rove, and he explored her delicious body as she grasped his penis and soaped it. He lifted her suddenly; her legs parted and the taut erection slid into her deeply as she gasped. Foucaud chuckled and held her bottom with both hands and moved, thrusting with the rampant member, lowering her into the water, which threshed about them as she squealed happily.

He laid her against the sloping side of the warm tub, still moving, her legs tight about him, moving . . . moving . . . She kissed him, unable to do anything but writhe and squirm— and then the blessed relief suddenly flooded her as she sighed, moaning . . .

She was on a bed, toweled dry, with Foucaud beside her, his untiring organ still deeply inside her. She curled close, loving his strong arms about her, lifting her lips for his kisses . . .

A candle was burning somewhere in the room and it was dark outside. How long had she been here? No, that wasn't important . . . She moved languidly, kneading him with her long, shapely legs, feeling the marvelous instrument swelling inside her . . . Tomorrow was years away . . .

Two weeks went by serenely. Twice Hap Stoker had come to the office to collect his pay. There had been no incidents, Stoker told Baily, nothing of any import anyway. His men had dealt with a few drunks and tossed some gamblers off the boat, at the captain's orders. But all in all the days were passing without problems.

There were no problems, Stoker said, because they were there ready for anything. Robbers knew better than to try them.

Privately Baily thought Dutch was probably still in one of the big towns, spending the stolen money. It was impossible to know how much the robbers had taken from passengers, because even though the passengers listed the items, they did not always tell the truth, for one reason or another. Gambling men in particular could not be trusted.

Dutch was constantly on Baily's mind. He deeply regretted allowing Dutch to know who he was. He should have dealt through a go-between. It was a measure of his entrance into crime. He was learning.

But one day, he was positive, as soon as Dutch thought about it, or as soon as someone suggested it to him, Dutch would begin blackmailing him.

He had to get rid of Dutch.

Lieutenant Foucaud received from St. Louis a list of stolen jewelry items, including watches, knickknacks, chains and even a few firearms. The lists were given to copyists and later distributed to the various stations throughout the city.

But Foucaud thought they had little chance of recovering any of the items. "I doubt very much if they would have been taken in the first place unless the thieves intended to sell them to someone who will melt down the metal, pry out the jewels and sell them piecemeal. They might even be shipped abroad for sale. You must remember that New Orleans is one of the great ports of the world."

Jessie sighed. "Then we must concentrate on Dutch himself."

"Yes, I think so. I'm sure the photograph of him will help us very much. Hundreds of copies are being made and sent around."

A reward was also offered, and in a week a letter arrived at the main police station. It was sent at once to Foucaud, who read it with mounting interest. It was on a scrap of paper, a crude scrawl; the writer knew where to find Dutch and wanted to know when he would receive the reward money.

Foucaud's men brought him in, an elderly black man who said his name was Jim. Jessica and Ki were present when Foucaud questioned the old man, first explaining that the reward would be forthcoming when Dutch was arrested and convicted by a court.

Jim said, "You mean they got to be a trial first?"

"Yes. That's right." Foucaud pointed out the wording on one of the flyers that bore Dutch's picture.

"I don't git no money now?"

"Not until the conviction," Foucaud told him.

"Then I best go on home." Jim got up. "When you—"

Foucaud pushed him gently back into the chair. "It doesn't work that way, Jim. You have to tell us where he is."

"I *got* to tell you?"

"Yes."

"But izzat fair? We ain't exchangin' nothing. I give you, but you don't give me."

Jessie said, "We'll give you something . . ."

"It's always done this way," Foucaud said. "You will be paid when we convict Dutch . . . if your information leads to his conviction."

"You got a lot of whens and ifs in that, mister policeman."

Foucaud smiled. "Some others make the rules. I just carry them out. Where is Dutch?"

Jim looked round at them and sighed. Jessie handed him twenty dollars. "Here's something anyway, Jim."

He bobbed his head to her. "Thankee, miss." He looked back at Foucaud. "I can't be sure about today, but two days ago he was at the Spotted Cat. I seen him there."

Ki said, "The Spotted Cat? What's that?"

"It's a brothel-saloon-gambling house." Foucaud thanked Jim and went with him to the door.

"A place for men only," Jessie said.

Foucaud came back. "Yes. You wouldn't get past the front door."

"Then I'll wait outside. When are you going there?"

"This evening. I'll have the place surrounded with patrolmen. The Cat is on two levels if I recall. We made some arrests there last year. If Dutch is inside, we'll find him."

Ki asked, "What about the others of his gang?"

38

Foucaud pursed his lips. "We're pretty sure we know two of their names, but not what they look like. Alley and Lyman—I wish we knew the others."

"They'll be there, with Dutch."

"I hope so."

Denis dressed in evening clothes. Ki had none, but dressed as conservatively as possible. Denis had also been able to obtain membership cards. "We have people who can manufacture these kinds of things," he said.

They presented themselves at the front door of the Cat and were passed in. Denis had changed his appearance considerably with a heavy mustache and darker brows. He thought it likely that one or more of the men he had arrested in other times might be present and would be delighted to unmask him.

But no one did. Ki viewed the place curiously. He had been in many New Orleans coffee houses and gambling palaces, but the Spotted Cat was a little different. It catered to two particular cravings, gambling and women. The lower floor was given over to card tables and other forms of gambling such as roulette and faro. There was an ornate stage at the end of the room, where daringly unclad dancers cavorted to the music of a small band. Other hostesses served coffee and drinks to the players.

The women in the life transacted their business upstairs. They met men on the main floor, perhaps had a drink or two with them, then went upstairs to the rooms.

Denis and Ki toured the floor without seeing Dutch. Ki said, "He isn't here. We'll have to go upstairs."

Denis scratched his chin. "But not without a girl." He gazed at the stairway. "And if we don't go in a room with her, she'll make a fuss."

Ki nodded. "And if we start opening doors at random, someone else will make a fuss."

"Yes. Not good."

"Is there only one stairway?"

"I think so. If Dutch is up there, he'll have to come down sometime."

39

"Then it might be smarter to stay down here and wait for him."

Foucaud sighed deeply. "Yes . . ."

But it was a long wait. They drifted from one table to another, watching the cardplayers, as others did. They put down a few bets here and there, always keeping a close watch on the stairs. No one seemed to pay them any particular attention.

By three o'clock in the morning, Dutch had still not appeared. The Cat was clearing out. Men put on overcoats and drifted away till only a dozen remained at the tables. The bandsmen packed up and the girls disappeared—and still Dutch did not come down the steps.

At four in the morning the club closed.

No one had come down the stairs for an hour. When Denis and Ki went outside to meet Jessica, it was with a sense of defeat. Had old Jim told them the truth? Or had Dutch given them the slip—knowingly or unknowingly?

Probably the latter, Foucaud thought.

★

Chapter 8

The small steamboat *Macon* was back in her berth, having made the round trip to Cairo, and would be leaving again in two days. Alley Trask made the reservations for the four of them. They were bound for Grogan.

Several hours before departure time, they went aboard the small stern-wheeler and occupied their tiny cabins. Then Dutch went on deck to watch the last of the cargo loading. The hatches were slammed down, and instead of a cannon, someone on the upper deck fired a pistol amid laughter. The boat trembled as the stern wheel beat the water and backed into the stream as the backing bells clanged. The steamboat slowed, shuddered, then slowly began to move forward as the paddle wheel reversed and beat the brown Mississippi to foam. Black smoke curled from the stacks, and Dutch grinned at the blur of faces on the levee.

They were off upriver again.

Was it about time to talk to Baily once more? A month had passed. Dutch lit a cigar and tossed the match overside. He leaned on the rail and puffed, thinking about Baily and the fifteen thousand dollars in the captain's safe. One of the boys, Cy or Alley, had noticed the safe and gotten into it. Dutch

41

was annoyed with himself—and had been since the incident. He should have kept the money and never gone back to see Baily. They might never see that much money again in one place. Yeah, he and the boys should have headed for New Orleans at once. To hell with Baily.

Well, live and learn. Live and get smart. Did they need Baily now? It had been different at first. Baily had shown him how to rob a steamboat. He hadn't even thought of it. Now he could rob any steamboat on the goddamn river . . . so long as it didn't have guards on board. A few did. You had to watch out for that.

Dutch grinned at the cigar. Well, Baily couldn't go to the police either. He was too involved. If they'd taken that fifteen thousand, Baily would have had to cry and swallow the loss. Nothing he could have done about it. Dutch hurled the half-smoked cigar into the river. Damn! If he'd realized that then!

He watched the cigar float past and disappear. Hell, Baily was very involved. And in that moment it occurred to him that Baily was really helpless!

Would he pay to remain a silent partner? Dutch had heard of blackmail, but it had never occurred to him that he might be in a position to exact money through that means.

But here was the perfect chance!

All he had to do was send Baily a note telling him where to ship the money. "Pay me or I'll go to the coppers with my story. They'll investigate you and find out I'm telling the truth. Then it'll be all over for you, Mr. Baily."

And I'll still be on the river. Somewhere.

Dutch frowned. But would they believe him over Baily, a big, important businessman? He didn't trust the law . . .

Dutch fished for another cigar. Should he tell the others about this? He scratched a match. Why should he? None of them knew Baily, not even his real name. He'd always called Baily Mr. Smith. Well, that had been Baily's idea. Now it could work in Dutch's favor—if he decided to do it.

He lit the cigar and puffed strongly. Could he trust the law to do it right?

If he did, how much would he ask for?

42

• • •

They got off the steamboat at Grogan. The boat hardly stopped for them, merely pulled up to the pilings and paused while they jumped across. Dutch glared up at the pale blur of faces in the wheelhouse as the boat pulled away and someone blew a whistle.

Plodding into town, they stopped at Simon Engle's deadfall for a few drinks. Simon wanted to know, "Where y'all been?"

"Down to New Orleans."

"What's the news?"

Alley chuckled. "News is, we still outa jail."

Simon looked them over. "Where's Lyman at?"

Dutch growled. "Lyman got hisself in a game and some picker shot 'im."

"Too bad. He dead, huh?"

"Deader'n four hunnerd iron frogs. Set up another drink, Simon."

It was late when they straggled down the road to the Rollins place. Everyone was in bed. Dutch lighted a lantern and slammed doors and got the house up.

Uncle Rudd and Aunt Mae rolled out. "Where the hell you drop from?"

"You got anything to eat?" Dutch demanded.

"Why can't you come home in daylight?"

"We come when the damn steamboats come."

Mae had some leftover beef and cornbread that she heated on the stove, and they sat around the table telling lies about New Orleans—where Rudd and Mae had never been.

Then Alley, Cy and Emory went out to the barn and bedded down. Dutch slept in the spare bed.

Roy Green was a wizened old-timer who had worked on the river all his life until he could no longer keep up with the younger set. Now he hung around the saloons, picking up what he could to keep belly and soul together. He had been sitting in a corner when Dutch and the others came in and were gabbing with Simon.

Roy slid out when they were all laughing and yelling and hurried off to see Karl Loder.

43

He got Karl out of bed. "Dutch's in town."

Karl smiled. "He alone?"

"Naw. He got three wi' him. Right now they sittin' in Simon's place."

Karl nodded, handed over some coins and turned Roy around. "You best git outa sight."

"I will." The old man hurried away.

Karl took down his squirrel gun, made sure it was loaded, put a new cap on the nipple, slung a powder flask over his shoulder and started along the road to the Rollins farm.

It was a five mile walk and he was too late. Lights were on in the shack and in the barn. He moved around the house peering in windows but could see nothing but shadows inside. He swore. There was no chance to draw a bead on Dutch.

He gave up and went back home.

He returned the next day, in the afternoon. He was sure Dutch would sleep till midday. He took up a station in a clump of trees several hundred yards from the house and made himself comfortable.

He watched old Rudd come out and putter around in the garden behind the house. Aunt Mae tossed out dishwater and later went to hang clothes on a line. Alley, Cy and Emory emerged from the barn, stretching and chattering, and disappeared into the house.

Nothing else happened for two hours.

Karl chewed on the jerky he had brought along. He had his route all planned. If he was lucky enough to shoot Dutch from this position, he would hustle down to the creek, which was fifty yards behind him. There was a boat pulled up there, and he would paddle across to the other side and trot through the woods and around to his own house. Without the boat, no one else could get across.

Finally someone came out onto the porch. Karl blinked and rubbed his eyes. Was it Dutch? It sure looked like him. Damn—his eyes weren't what they used to be. He laid the long barrel of the rifle along a grass hummock and pulled the stock tight against his shoulder, drawing a bead on the distant figure. He allowed for distance, but there was no wind at all.

His finger tightened on the trigger, taking up the slack. He was sure it was Dutch.

Then he relaxed his finger as the figure walked to the far end of the porch, hands in his pockets. Karl growled under his breath. Then the figure walked back to a chair and sat down.

Karl grinned and pulled the stock close. Dutch was rocking back and forth but directly facing him. He squeezed the trigger again delicately. The butt slammed against his shoulder all at once as the gun went off. He saw the distant figure suddenly topple backward, legs flying. Dutch fell in a tangle, the chair upside down. Nothing moved.

Karl chuckled aloud. He watched for a moment, then turned and hurried for the creek, hearing shouts.

It would probably take them a while to figure out where the shot had come from. He clambered into the boat, shoved off from the bank and paddled across the creek, some fifty feet. On the far side he jumped out and pulled the boat up, concealing it in brush. He stepped back into the trees and took a moment to reload the rifle, grinning happily. They must be running around, yelling and swearing . . .

Good-bye, Dutch.

They gathered in the kitchen an hour after noon while Aunt Mae dished out grits and homemade bread. Rudd asked, "How long you boys figgerin' on stayin'?"

"Maybe a week," Dutch replied. He dug into his pocket and laid a gold eagle on the table in front of Mae. The others did the same, and she scooped them up, smiling. They could stay as long as they wished.

Dutch wanted to talk about boats. Rudd said he knew everyone in town who owned one. Dutch said it would be handy as hell for him and the boys to own their own steamer. Nothing big, a small boat, say twenty feet, would do fine. Then they could run up and down the river whenever they wanted.

"You ain't rivermen," Rudd said.

"Hell, don't need to be for makin' short trips. We know enough. And Emory here, he's good with engines. That's the most thing we got to know."

Emory nodded. He was a tinkerer.

Cy yawned and got up to wander out to the porch. He was uninterested in the discussion. Dutch would take care of things. He lit a cigar and walked from one end of the porch to the other, looking at the distant blue hills, wishing he was back in New Orleans. That was the fun place to be. He sighed and sat in the chair and began rocking.

Jessica and Ki took the steamboat *Hendon* upriver to St. Louis and went at once to see Aunt Lydia. She was still in the hospital, sitting up in a chair, her arm and shoulder heavily bandaged. It was knitting, she told them, but slowly. More slowly than the doctors had thought it would.

But she was cheerful. The pain was largely gone. "I may be going home in a week," she said. "Then I'll find a place to sit in the sun . . ."

Jessie took the doctor aside. He told her, "We had to operate again. The bullet tore her up considerably and there was great danger of gangrene . . ."

"But she's all right now?"

"Yes. She's on the road to recovery . . . but it's slow. Her general health is good, but she's not as strong as could be wished."

"Make certain she gets every care," Jessie said. "No matter what it costs. I will see to it."

"Certainly, Miss Starbuck."

Next they went to see Sergeant Tyler. Jessica sent a note to him, and he sent the messenger back to say he would meet them in an hour in the park behind the police station.

When he appeared he was in civilian clothes and smilingly shook hands with Ki and took off his hat to Jessie. "Where have you two been?"

"Downriver," Ki said. "Is anything happening here?"

"Yes. We finally got the photograph of Dutch copied and pasted up around town. But so far it's brought us nothing but a few confessions from bums and persons weak in the head."

"The picture has been distributed in New Orleans also," Jessie said.

"Good. I've sent some to various river towns, so Dutch ought to see his face staring back at him wherever he goes.

46

Let's hope he stays on the river. He could get on a horse and head west, you know."

"He might—if he feels threatened enough."

"It's a mighty long river," Tyler said. "We're doing what we can, but we have limited resources to chase down crime not directly under our noses. There's enough to keep us busy right here in St. Louis, as you can imagine."

"We appreciate what you're doing," Jessie told him.

"How's your aunt?"

"She's recovering . . ."

"That's good."

Ki said, "You've had no reports from anyone about what haunts or friends Dutch might have here in the city?"

"None at all. I really doubt if Dutch has been here except to come and go quickly." Sergeant Tyler fiddled with his watch chain. "He's not a big city crook, so he may feel uncomfortable here. I hope he does."

They returned to the hotel and were surprised to find a note waiting for them. It was from Lydia, asking them to come and see her when they could.

They hurried out to the street and got a hack, fearing the wound had taken a turn for the worse. But it was not that. Lydia had something to tell them.

"I've been thinking a lot about the robbery in the last week or so . . . Dreaming about it too . . ."

"What is it, Aunt Lydia?"

"Well, child, as you might imagine, I've had many a nightmare about that time—"

"Hasn't the doctor given you sedatives?"

"Oh yes. But I've had some very bad dreams nevertheless—and some in the daytimes too. And for a long while I thought they were just dreams . . . bad dreams."

Jessie glanced at Ki. "What do you mean?"

Lydia took a long breath, her good hand gently rubbing up and down the bandages. "I thought for a long time they were just wild dreams, my seeing those men."

"Seeing them?"

"Yes, child. Seeing them. Two of them. If I saw them again, I know I'd recognize them."

47

★

Chapter 9

At the shot and the smashing sounds from the porch, Dutch and the others rushed out. Cy was on his back, arms flung out, one foot caught in the rungs of the upturned chair. There was a bloody hole in his chest. Dutch felt for a pulse. There was none.

"Jeez Christ!" Rudd said. "Who done that?"

Aunt Mae said, "Somebody after Cy?"

"Hell no." Emory growled. "Not Cy. They thought he was Dutch."

Dutch stared at him, and Emory said, "Well, you's the one the reward is out for."

"That's right," Alley agreed. He frowned around the landscape. "Where'd the shot come from?"

Rudd pointed. "Over there . . ." He ran down the steps and jogged toward the trees; the others followed.

Rudd quickly found where someone had spent time under a clump of small pines. "He waited here till Cy came out on the porch. Then he shot 'im." He looked around and walked toward the creek. "He prob'ly went this way . . ."

"How deep is that crick?" Alley asked.

"Too deep to wade it. He hadda have a boat." Rudd examined the shoreline. "Yeah—here's where he pulled a boat up. See, it's still wet. See them marks?" He stared across the creek. "I reckon we'll find us a boat over there in the brush."

"Whose boat?"

"It could be anybody's up and down the creek. Findin' the boat ain't gonna point out the shooter."

They went back to the house. Rudd put out a bottle of moonshine, and they had drinks all round, moodily. Dutch sat by the fire, brooding. Who had shot Cy? It could have been Karl Loder. He knew that Karl had made threats against him—several people had told him so.

But Emory was probably right. Someone had seen Cy on the porch and shot the wrong man.

He turned from the fire. "Lissen, whoever shot Cy might maybe claim the reward—"

"The reward is on you," Rudd objected.

"He don't know he shot Cy 'stead of me. So if he tries to collect, maybe we can grab him."

Alley shook his head. "He'd have to have the body to collect. The law ain't dumb enough to pay out money on somebody's say so."

"That's right," Rudd agreed.

"Well, we can give 'im Cy and say it's me."

"Hell no. Cy don't look nothing like you."

Dutch growled. "The shooter thought so."

"Sure, maybe, from a distance."

Alley said musingly, "There is one thing . . ."

"What?"

"We been mentioning the reward. Why don't we give it out that Dutch is dead? Then maybe they'll stop looking for him and us."

Dutch grinned. "That's a great idee. But first we shoot that sombitch, Loder."

That evening they wrapped the body of Cy in an old blanket, laid it in the bed of Rudd's buckboard and hauled it into the woods a mile or so.

49

Taking turns by lantern light, they dug a deep hole and then they lowered the body down and covered it up. They stomped down the dirt, then scattered leaves and rocks on the grave till it looked as if the ground had never been disturbed.

The next morning, Emory, the best hand at writing, scratched a letter to the nearest newspaper, the Wilkins County *Journal*. The letter stated that Dutch Rollins had been shot from ambush and killed near the town of Grogan and that he had been buried there. His killer had not been found.

Rudd walked into town and posted the letter.

In New Orleans Lieutenant Foucaud concluded that since no one had come forward with information about Dutch—his picture and the reward notice were everywhere—then Dutch was probably not in the city.

He went back alone, in late evening, to the Spotted Cat, wearing his disguise, and did not find him. Not one of his informants had heard a word concerning Dutch. If he were in New Orleans, he was holed up somewhere, not showing his face.

Foucaud doubted even that.

An enterprising newspaper reporter who happened to be wooing one of the hospital nurses, listened, quite by accident, to a conversation in one of the wards. He squeezed out of the nurse the fascinating rumor that Lydia Franklin, a patient who had been shot by the Dutch Rollins gang, could identify two of the robbers!

This was front page news! And he printed it.

It was also the first break in the case, and it brought Lieutenant Ware to the hospital, steaming. He demanded to know why Lydia had withheld the information so long.

She tried to tell him that she had not really believed herself that she had seen them—and could remember what she had seen. The doctors had to warn the policeman not to shout.

Lydia said, in a very small voice, that it was only when she had began to recover that things began to sort themselves out—

what was real and what was not.

The doctor said she had had a very great shock and it would not help to be shouted at. Lieutenant Ware calmed down, obviously not believing her, but there was little he could do and he finally left, almost pushed out by two doctors.

However, he placed a uniformed policeman at her door.

Jessie and Ki were startled to read in the newspapers that Lydia could identify two of the murderous thieves. The newsmen were more interested in sales than her life.

Jessie went at once to the hospital officials, and they agreed that Lydia could be discharged the very second the doctors said she could go. Jessica would put her in a safe, well-guarded place until the Dutch Rollins gang was behind bars or dead.

Unfortunately the news item was picked up by most papers, including the Wilkins County *Journal*, and Dutch and the others read it with much interest.

"They got a picture of me and they know two of you," he said.

"They don't say which two," Alley remarked. "Maybe Cy and Lyman."

"When did you ever have that kinda luck? Prob'ly you and Emory."

"Whoever it is, it's bad," Alley growled. "We ought to shut her up."

Emory studied the article. "It says she's in the hospital in St. Louis. She's just an old woman. Ought to be easy to shut her mouth."

The newspaper story was bad enough, but on the inside page was the picture of Dutch! He was astounded, staring at it. "Damn them—they got no right t'print that!"

Emory asked, "Where'd it come from?"

"They took it at Reidsville when I was there years ago. They took pitchers of ever'body."

"It still looks like you, Dutch."

Rudd said, "Well, he got a little more hair then . . ."

Dutch glared at them and crumpled the paper and tossed it into the fire.

Alley suggested, "You oughta grow a mustache or a beard, Dutch. Change your face."

That was an idea. Dutch felt his chin. It was already started.

One of his informants sent Stoker a wire saying that Dutch Rollins had been seen in a gambling house in New Orleans.

Stoker took passage there at once, not terribly happy to see flyers bearing Dutch's picture pasted here and there. Someone else might get to him first.

The gambling house in question turned out to be the Spotted Cat, and Stoker discovered that it was much more than just a gambling casino. It was also a high-class brothel with a dozen or more girls in attendance.

He showed the picture to everyone who would look, but none of the men employed by the Cat recognized Dutch. Stoker did not believe them but had to accept it.

He then took the girls, one by one, paying their fees. None of the girls would discuss the picture—or anything else—without money up front.

But at last he found a girl who said she remembered Dutch. "He was here half a dozen times, I guess."

"Where is he now?"

"How the hell would I know?"

"I mean did he ever say anything about where he would go from here?"

"No."

"He never discussed anything with you?"

"Sure." She laughed. "He discussed what we was gonna do in bed."

"And that's all?"

"What the hell else would he discuss?"

Stoker got nowhere.

He gave it up and left the Cat. Playing detective wasn't as easy as he had thought. The trouble was, Dutch was a small-time crook. If he'd been famous—notorious—people would have remembered him; he'd have been easy to trace.

Stoker went into the streets and began methodically going down a list of hotels near the Cat. It took an entire day to find where Dutch and the others had stayed.

But he learned nothing from it. He could not see the room Dutch had occupied, because someone else was in it. He wasn't sure what seeing it would do anyway.

The clerks could not tell him anything he did not already know.

He was at a dead end.

★
Chapter 10

Johnson Baily was startled to see the picture of Dutch pasted up on the streets and in front of saloons. He hadn't known there was a photograph of him in existence. It was unsettling. What if the police caught Dutch—and he talked.

And he would certainly talk. Dutch had not impressed him as the brave, hardy, stoic type. If the police took him into a padded room and beat him, Dutch would spill all he knew. And if they caught him, the police would certainly beat him. They always did.

Dutch would tell them he robbed Baily steamboats at Baily's orders.

Would the coppers believe such a story? If they beat it out of Dutch, they would probably believe it . . . no matter how bizarre they thought it.

And if the police dug into the story, investigated Baily, they would discover the connection between him and Elliot Scully.

That would be disastrous.

He had to stop Dutch's mouth—somehow. He sent a message to Hap Stoker: the bounty on Dutch was increased to one thousand dollars!

● ● ●

Barring any kind of setback, which was unlikely, the doctor told Jessica, Aunt Lydia could be discharged from the hospital in a week. She was doing fine and was expected to continue. He would want to look in on her about once a month, he said, just to be on the safe side.

Jessie employed an agent, who found a furnished house on Deerfield Street. It was a small house with a high fence and a garden; there would be excellent privacy, and Jessie would hire a housekeeper, a nurse and a guard.

Aunt Lydia lived in Memphis, but she would stay near the hospital for several more months to make certain there were no complications.

In the meantime the search for Dutch and the gang went on. They had little to use but the picture, and though it was widely circulated, it brought no real results.

When they talked to him, Sergeant Tyler did not hold out a great deal of hope. "Our files are full of information and material on thieves and murderers we may never catch. All police departments have the same. What we need of course is a central clearing house for every sort of criminal information, so it can be sent where it's needed. There are a lot of towns along the river, and everywhere, that have information we could use—some probably about Dutch—but we'll never see it."

"A central file," Jessie said, musing. "I wonder if it'll ever happen."

"The politicians will never vote for it," Tyler said. "It's too sensible."

Rudd talked to a dozen men in the town who had boats, and located a small steamer that the owner was willing to part with. The boat was the *Cynthy*. It was named after his wife, the owner said. He had bought it some ten years back, to ferry passengers across the river and back. He had done well, but when his wife died, he lost interest and decided to sell the boat and go sit on his porch.

Dutch and Emory went with Rudd to look at the boat. It had been hauled out of the water and a workman was sanding her bottom. *Cynthy* was about twenty-five feet long, had a cabin below decks and a small pilothouse. Another workman was replacing several paddles on the stern wheel.

The boiler had been cleaned and scoured. Emory snaked himself partly inside and examined it for rust, finding none. The boat had been well cared for. It needed paint topside, but that was a minor matter. They would paint it a dark color . . .

Dutch, Emory and the boat's owner haggled over price for an hour or two but finally agreed, and when the workmen were finished, the boat was dragged back into the water.

On their first trip upstream, they made the run to Cairo and tied up there nearly a week. They provisioned the boat and painted it a dark brown with black trim.

That done, they held a council of war in the cabin at night. They were very low on money. Buying the boat had taken most of what they had. They knew only one way to get more quickly.

In the morning they began the run downriver. They steamed to a point below Memphis and found a lonely cove near a wood yard on the Arkansas side. They tied the boat securely under the trees; it blended perfectly. A chance passerby would have to come within a few yards of it to realize there was a boat close by.

The woodhawk was an older man sitting by the fire in his shack. They crowded in, bound the man's feet and waited for the next steamboat.

It was a three-hour wait before a boat, bound upriver, nudged into the pilings. Emory and Alley lighted the wood baskets at the boat's whistle, and when the crew tied her off, the three of them went aboard with pistols and a grain sack. "All right, folks, line up. Don't do nothing foolish and nobody gits hurt."

They found no safe on board, and when they had gone through the crew and passengers, they disappeared into the gloom.

It had been a very good night. They had a good haul in jewelry, watches and other items, and about a thousand dollars in cash. Dutch was all for going up to St. Louis at once.

"We'll find us another fence. We need one at each end of the river."

After some argument, the others agreed.

They waited till morning, then set out with Alley at the wheel, all of them feeling as if they had the world by the tail. They had their own steamboat, and their method of replenishing funds was obviously foolproof. The law would never catch them.

They pushed into a berth on the St. Louis levee and made fast. Dutch and Alley Trask went ashore and nosed along saloon row, asking questions, buying drinks and listening. Was there anyone who bought and sold goods . . . ?

One name came up several times—Purvis Zale. Evidently he was in the business of buying and selling anything that could turn a dollar. Not necessarily an honest dollar, just a dollar.

He had a hole-in-the-wall shop where he did over-the-counter business behind a wire cage. He was often out in his wagon, they were told, drumming up trade here, there, everywhere. He was slippery as a greased eel, people said, but he paid off in cash and could keep his mouth shut. It was thought he had a warehouse full of items, but no one knew where it was.

They went to the address and found him in.

Purvis was a skinny little gent with an untended beard and a bowler hat. And a pistol belted around over his coat. He was sitting behind a metal cage with another pistol at his elbow. He looked them over as they came through the door. "Howdy, folks. What kin I do f'you?"

"We got a few things t'sell," Dutch said, gazing around. Every sort of article was hanging from the walls or stacked around them, with barely enough room to walk to the cage.

Purvis said, "You got something to show me?"

Dutch dug in his pocket and brought out some of the unmarked jewelry. He laid it on the wooden counter, where the gems sparkled in the poor light.

Purvis moved a lamp closer, screwed a glass into one eye and leaned in to examine the stones. "Hmmmmmm." He smiled at Dutch. "You brought this batch to the right person, friend. I'm knowed as Honest Purvis. What you want for the lot?"

"What'll you give?" Dutch countered.

Purvis took the glass from his eye and nudged the pile of gems with a little finger. "Is this all you got?"

"No. There's lots more."

"Ahhh. Where is it?"

"Safe."

"Ahha." Honest Purvis regarded them, head on one side like a brown, scraggly bird. He scratched his chin and looked curious, staring at Dutch. "You been in here before, friend?"

"No."

"Ummmm. I sure seen you someplace. Did we meet somewheres?"

"I don't think so."

Purvis sighed. "All right. When do I see the rest of what you got to sell?"

Dutch said, "How about tomorrow?"

"How did you hear about me?"

"We ast around. We lissen good."

Alley said, "We's looking for a honest man."

Purvis smiled. "That's me. Honest as the day is long. Do you know anybody I know?"

Alley shook his head. "We strangers in town."

Dutch had an inspiration. "We know Isaac Kupper in New Orleans."

"Ahhhhh. You done business with him?"

"Lots of business."

Purvis's attitude seemed to change. "All right, friends. You come in tomorrow mornin' before noon. I give you as good as Isaac does. Bring what you got."

"We'll be here," Dutch said.

"And no word to nobody." Purvis put a finger over his thin lips.

"Nobody." Dutch nodded.

Hap Stoker got Baily's wire and took the next steamboat north. He was positive Dutch was not in New Orleans.

When the boat arrived at New Madrid, he bought a newspaper at the dock. Another steamboat had been robbed south of Memphis, at a wood yard. Three men had done the job and got away in the dark.

It was exactly the way Dutch Rollins and his gang worked. But three men? There should be four. Had something happened to one of the gang? He could be sick in bed somewhere . . . or lost his nerve and quit.

Or maybe it wasn't Dutch at all. He wasn't the only criminal on the river, God knew. Stoker folded the paper and laid it aside, fishing for a stogie. No, it *was* Dutch. Stoker was seeing a girl named Amy in St. Louis, and he would bet one of her tits on it.

Robbed south of Memphis . . . that meant Dutch and the gang might go either way, up or down river. Stoker wished he knew more about Dutch. How could you second-guess a shadow?

When he had closed and padlocked the shop, Honest Purvis went next door to Mitch Auer's saloon and sat for a while nursing a glass of beer. On the backbar was a flyer, and he squinted at it, then got out his specs and put them on.

The flyer was headed by the word "REWARD!" Underneath was a picture of the man who had been in Purvis's shop only hours ago. So that was where he'd seen him! On a reward poster. His name was Dutch Rollins and he was a robber-murderer.

With booty to sell.

Purvis sipped the beer, recalling the newspaper items he'd seen. Dutch was credited with half a dozen robberies along the river. They ought to have quite a pile of items to get rid of . . . if they had not sold most of it already to Isaac in New Orleans.

Well, Isaac was a long way off. Probably Dutch and his gang had done jobs on the way to St. Louis and might have a very interesting pile of goods. Honest Purvis rubbed his hands together, itching to get his fingers on them. His home was a shabby two rooms, a sitting-bedroom and a small kitchen with a hand pump.

He ordinarily wore two revolvers, one under his coat and one strapped around it. He sat down, unloaded and cleaned them both carefully and then loaded them again. There was thousands of dollars worth of articles, including gems and cash, in Purvis's shop. The guns he carried on his person and the ones in the shop under the counter were his insurance.

He had been robbed once long ago, before he had put up the metal screen, and he had vowed it would never happen again. There was no way a man on the outside could reach under the screen and across the counter. Not only had Purvis put up the screen, but he'd lined the wooden siding under the counter with heavy sheet iron that no bullet could penetrate.

All he had to do was duck down, and no robber could touch him . . . or his valuables.

He did not really fear Dutch, even though he knew the man was a robber and a killer, because Dutch needed him, and men like him, to dispose of the items he acquired.

But Purvis never took chances if he could avoid them. When he went to the shop the next morning, he laid a double-action Colt revolver on the shelf, within easy reach, just below the counter where Dutch would place his goods.

★

Chapter 11

Dutch and Alley Trask arrived at the narrow little shop at eleven o'clock in the morning. When they entered, Purvis, from behind the screen, asked them to lock the door and turn the sign so it read CLOSED. "Now we won't be disturbed," he said.

Dutch was carrying a black leather valise. He snapped back the lock and dumped the glittering contents on the wide counter before Purvis, whose eyes rounded. It was more than he'd expected to see.

He smiled at Dutch and began poking through the pile, sorting out the items, just as Isaac had done.

Alley leaned on the counter, and Dutch lit a cigar and watched. He and the others had spent a few hours prying stones from settings, rings, earrings and brooches. Purvis moved all the loose stones aside, now and then using a glass to examine one or another more closely. He hummed softly to himself as he worked.

When he had put aside the chains and watches and made neat piles of the rest, he got out a pad and pencil and began figuring, making notations and pushing aside one pile, then the next. When he had toted up his figures, he cocked his head, made an adjustment, then wrote a number on a bit of paper and pushed it toward his visitors.

Dutch frowned at it, glanced at Alley and said, "Add a little something to that, Purvis."

Purvis straightened, looked as if he'd been stabbed and closed his eyes. He sighed deeply, took a while to consider, then finally jotted another figure.

Dutch insisted it was still too low, and Purvis adjusted it again. They finally came to an agreement and Honest Purvis counted out the cash. Dutch pocketed it and they nodded to each other. Dutch picked up the empty valise, and he and Alley went out, turning the sign around.

Purvis smiled at their backs and rubbed his hands together. A good morning's work.

The next order of business was the woman in the hospital. The newspapers had obligingly told them which hospital, and Dutch and Alley hired a hack to drive them there.

They saw a series of long, low buildings painted white. Which one was she in?

Dutch said, "You go in and ask at the main office. See if you can find out where she is. Tell them you're a relative just got in town and seen the newspapers."

"What's her name again?"

"The paper said she was Lydia Franklin. You'll be her cousin."

Alley nodded. "Lydia Franklin. Is my name Franklin too?"

"Of course it is. John or Joe—"

"All right." Alley followed the several neat black-on-white signs to the main office, brushed at his rough clothes, took off his hat and entered.

A man with spectacles, sitting at a desk piled with papers, asked his business.

Alley said, "I come to see about Miz Franklin. She's a cousin. She an' my mum was sisters."

The man nodded, got up and looked through a cabinet and returned with a blue file. He leafed through it. "Miz Lydia Franklin?"

"Yes."

"You can't see her."

"Why not, dammit! She's my cousin."

"It doesn't matter. She's not allowed to have visitors."

"She isn't? Why not?"

"Because the police say so. That's why." The man was holding the file loosely, and on the side of it in black letters was the notation "L-82." He returned the file to the cabinet and sat down again.

Alley said, "No way I c'n see her? Is she in bed?"

"I don't know. I can tell her you were here, though. What's your name?"

"John Franklin." He saw the man write it down and went to the door, wondering if the woman had a cousin named John.

He met Dutch on the street and related what the clerk had said.

Dutch said, "L-82, huh? Izzat her room number?"

"Might be. We could ast somebody . . ."

There were a number of buggies, a few carriages and some wagons on the street. They leaned against a wagon and waited. When a man in a white coat came out, Dutch stopped him.

"Can you tell me where L-82 is?"

The man nodded. "See that end building? The room is about halfway down. Those are private rooms, though, in that ward."

Dutch thanked him.

The hospital went through to the next street, which was shaded by trees. If they had to get out of the L building in a hurry, they might go that way.

Alley said, "How we going to get into the building in the first place?"

"We need some of them white coats."

Alley snapped his fingers.

They bought white coats at a clothing emporium in town and went back to the hospital after dark. The street in front of the hospital was crowded with buggies and carriages and people coming and going, many with flowers and packages.

Dutch and Alley donned the white coats in the shadow of a large carriage, then walked to the end building, dropped their hats on the grass and opened the door. Inside was a desk, a

63

center hallway and half a dozen people talking and bustling about. A man in a white jacket pushed a laden cart into the hall, and Dutch signed to Alley and followed.

When they reached L-82 Dutch halted and they looked about. No one was near them; the man with the cart had disappeared into a room. Alley drew his pistol and cocked it. Dutch nodded, pulled his own revolver, opened the door and they rushed in.

The room was vacant.

"Shit!" Dutch said. "They taken her out."

"Maybe she got well." Alley put the gun away.

"You sure about the room number?"

"Positive."

Dutch sighed. "Then we too late."

The report, printed in the Wilkins County *Journal*, that Dutch Rollins had been killed in an ambush, was picked up by most other papers in the area.

Jessica said, "Ambushed by whom? It doesn't say."

"Well, remember Karl Loder said he was going to shoot Dutch the first chance he got. Maybe he got one."

"Maybe . . ."

Ki smiled. "You want to go to Grogan to confirm it?"

"Or deny it—yes."

"Will you believe it when you see his grave?"

"No. Not until they dig him up and open the box."

Ki laughed. "All right. I'll make the arrangements. You want to go tomorrow?"

"As soon as possible."

He bought tickets on the *Humber*, a side-wheel steamer leaving in the middle of the morning. They were on the levee an hour before sailing time to put their things in the staterooms. Jessica relaxed in the lounge with coffee and small cakes while Ki roamed the decks. She felt in her bones that Dutch was alive and they'd find nothing in Grogan, but they had to make the effort, turn over every stone.

When the steamboat finally backed out and started downstream, Ki came in and sat by her. "A wager . . ."

"What?"

"Ten dollars says there is no grave with Dutch's name on it."

She smiled. "No bet. But what are the possibilities that Dutch advertised his own death?"

"Very good, I'd say. If they believed it, the law would put his file on the bottom of the stack."

"But we won't."

They were the only passengers to get off the boat at the lonely Grogan dock. There was a three-room hotel in town, and they got rooms and inquired about the cemetery. It turned out to be a plot on a gentle hillside at the south edge of town. They hired a buggy and drove there before dark.

There was no new grave in the entire area, and no headstone with Dutch's name on it. They made certain by looking at every one. There were five with the name Rollins, but the dates were in the past.

Ki said, "Of course he could have been ambushed somewhere else—the newspaper was vague—and buried somewhere else."

"Do you believe it?"

Ki sighed. "No . . ."

When they returned to town, Ki asked the hotel clerk, "Is there another cemetery in the area?"

"Nope, that's it. Unless you want to go to Wilkins, but it's maybe a hunnerd mile over a bad road."

They looked in at the local undertaker's office. The man called himself Dr. Royer. He was slim, aged and toothless, playing solitaire on a casket. No, he had buried no one in the last two weeks. But he was expecting several . . .

Jessie asked, "What about Dutch Rollins?"

The old man crackled. "He ain't dead—that I know of." He squinted at them. "You know something I don't?"

"No," Ki assured him. "It's just that there was a story in the newspapers that he was ambushed and killed."

"Oh, that. I read it. That fool paper over to Wilkins—they don't know they ass about what happens here. You can't believe nothing they print."

"Have you seen Dutch since the story?"

"No . . ."

"But you think it's untrue?"

The undertaker shrugged. "Yeah, I think so."

They went to call on Karl Loder and found him sitting by an open window facing the road. He had a shotgun and two pistols handy. When he recognized them, he waved them in. "I waitin' for Dutch," he said.

He had two other friends as well armed, watching the back door and the windows. Dutch would get a hot reception if he called.

"Why are you expecting him?" Jessie asked.

Karl grinned. "Because he thinks I took a shot at him and killed Cy."

"Why would he think that?"

"Because somebody shot Cy Carew on Dutch's porch and me and Dutch is enemies."

"But why would he think you'd shoot Cy instead of him?"

Karl scratched his neck. "Because he was shot from a distance and maybe I thought he was Dutch." He kept one eye on the road. "That's what I hear anyways. What you folks doing back here?"

"Looking for Dutch."

"Well, he kind of dropped out of sight—since he bought his boat."

Jessie was surprised. "A boat? What kind of boat?"

"A steamer. He bought old Harris's boat, *Cynthy*. Small steamboat. Harris used to ferry folks back and forth across the river."

Ki asked, "A small steamboat?"

"Yeah, maybe thirty feet long. He can tie up anywheres. The damn thing will run on wet grass too . . . run up any old crick. That's why we settin' by the windows. Dutch could show up any time."

Ki looked at Jessie. "Or he could be anywhere from the mouth of the Mississippi to Fort Benton on the edge of Canada."

Karl nodded. "That's right. Anywhere in about three thousand miles."

Ki said, "So there's one less of the Dutch Rollins gang . . ."

Karl smiled.

"He's not buried in the cemetery outside of town."

"Well, Dutch and them prob'ly hauled 'im back in the woods and planted 'im. Then they give out that story about Dutch bein' dead. Nobody around here believes a damn word of it."

They thanked Karl, wished him good luck and went out to the buggy. As they drove back to town Ki said, "Did Karl shoot Cy on the porch?"

"Of course he did. He thought it was Dutch."

"So he knows Dutch will come for him one of these days."

Jessie shrugged. "He doesn't seem much afraid of Dutch. But Dutch still has three men, doesn't he?"

"Well, there were only three altogether in the holdup near Simcoe. *If* that was Dutch and the gang."

"Maybe he's lost two men . . ."

"That's possible."

★

Chapter 12

Hap Stoker learned from Johnson Baily that the town of Grogan was a hangout of Dutch Rollins's. As he smoked a stogie, and gazed at the mighty river, he considered the fact that he wasn't far from the little town now. Why not go there? He might pick up something useful.

He bought passage on the next packet boat that arrived and got off at the Grogan landing early in the morning. Neither of the two saloons in town were open yet, so he sat on a bench and waited. What a dumpy little burg! What kind of people would live in a little backwater dismal like this?

When he saw the restaurant open, he got up, went across the street and ate eggs and grits with bitter coffee, ignoring the stares of other customers. He was used to curious eyes because of his bulk.

He sat where he could watch the street, and when the first saloon opened, he went across and entered to lean on the bar, the only customer in the place. He motioned to the bartender.

"Gimme beer . . ." He fished out a cigar. "You know Dutch Rollins?"

"Ever'body knows Dutch."

"Is he in town?"

"Don't know."

"You hear all the talk. Why don't you know?"

The bartender stopped polishing a glass. "How the hell I know what Dutch does?"

Stoker leaned across the bar and grabbed the man by the shirtfront, pulling him close. "Don't get smart wi' me—I bust you up, hear?"

The bartender stared at Stoker, who gradually released his grip and settled back. "Where does Dutch live?"

"Down the road a piece." The man inclined his head.

"How'll I know the house?"

"It got a big tulip tree out front."

"Dutch lives there?"

"He stays there when he's in town. Born there, I guess."

"His folks still live there?"

The bartender nodded. "Aunt and uncle. His other folks is gone. What you want Dutch for?"

Stoker finished his beer. "Just t'see him about some business." He slid the glass across the bar, turned and went out.

The bartender hurried to the back and whistled over a fence. A teenage boy was hammering something at a bench. He looked around at the whistle. "Yeah, Sam?"

"Git on your pony and ride around the back way to Rudd's place. Tell 'im a stranger's come to collect the reward on Dutch. He's a big sombitch."

"He on his way to Rudd's now?"

"Just left here. Hurry up." He tossed a coin to the boy, who caught it with a grin.

Rudd was outside in the vegetable garden with a hoe when he saw the boy gallop the pony across a field toward him. He leaned on the hoe and watched the other rein in.

"Somebody comin' to git Dutch."

"Who told you that?"

"Sam, at the Two Barrels. Says the feller's a big one."

"Dutch ain't here."

The boy shrugged. He turned the horse, waved and galloped off again. Rudd stared after him. Somebody after the reward? He dropped the hoe and went into the house. In the parlor, he

69

took down a 56–52 Spencer carbine and headed for the front porch.

Mae said, "What you doing?"

"Feller coming to shoot Dutch."

"Not here he ain't . . ."

Rudd stepped onto the porch and leaned out to look down the road. Nobody was in sight.

He sat on a rocker, the carbine across his knees. In a dozen minutes he saw the man in the distance, plodding along the dusty road. A huge man all right.

When the stranger turned in toward the porch, Rudd stood. "You kin stop there."

The stranger halted and frowned at him, then took a step.

Rudd cocked the carbine by springing the lever. At the sound, the man halted again. "I'm lookin' for Dutch Rollins."

"Dutch ain't been around here for a month."

"That's not what I hear."

Rudd made a face. "I don't care what you hear. You git along." He waved the muzzle toward the road.

"Maybe Dutch's in the house . . ."

Rudd moved to point the carbine directly at the big man. "I got eight reasons here why you ain't comin' in." He tapped the stock. "You take my meanin'?"

Stoker glared at the round muzzle of the gun. It looked very large and dark, and the old man with his finger on the trigger looked capable.

He said, "You expect to see Dutch soon?"

"Maybe—and maybe not."

Stoker frowned at the old man for a minute. "You tell 'im that Mr. Baily wants to see him. He knows who that is."

"Mr. Baily?"

"Yes." Stoker turned and went back to the road. It was a long shot, but if Dutch came to St. Louis looking to meet Baily, there might be a very good chance to center him. It might be better than chasing Dutch up and down the river.

Four days later Alley Trask nosed *Cynthy* into the bank along the Grogan waterfront. They tied her up and stepped ashore.

In the Two Barrels, Dutch learned about Stoker. Sam said, "Big sombitch in here lookin' for you, Dutch. He after the reward."

Rudd told him the same thing. "Big feller here lookin' for you. Said to tell you Mr. Baily wants t'see you. You know somebody by that name?"

"Ummm." Baily wanted to see him? He had no intention of going back to the agreement he had with Baily. He didn't need Baily anymore, and Baily ought to know that.

So why would Baily want to see him?

Was it a plot—to shut his mouth? He'd go to meet Baily and instead he'd meet half a dozen gunmen . . . ?

He had thought of blackmailing Baily and had done nothing about it. Maybe now was a good time to do it. If Baily was itchy about what he, Dutch, knew, he might pay up quick.

The more he thought about it, the more he was convinced. Baily wanted to shut him up—forever. And it angered him. He had played fair with Baily—in his ignorance. Hadn't he given back the fifteen thousand dollars in cash they'd found in the *Majesta*'s safe? He wouldn't do that now.

Maybe he ought to do something about Baily. Things could work both ways.

And the more he thought about *that*, the better he felt. Baily considered himself so mighty and high-up. A Colt's revolver would even the score with him damn fast.

Alley and Emory wanted to return to New Orleans. They had money to spend and the Crescent City was very attractive to them. They knew nothing about Baily anyway, except that he was someone called "Mr. Smith," whom they no longer needed.

They spent several days in Grogan, mostly drinking. There were no painted women at all in the town, and by the third day Dutch had made up his mind. He would go up to St. Louis and somehow get a meeting with Baily alone. Then one of two things would happen: Baily would give him blackmail money—or he would kill Baily.

Alley and Emory would take the *Cynthy* downriver to the big city and come back to Grogan in two or three weeks.

71

Many of the posters with the picture of Dutch Rollins on them that were pasted up about the town were fading, torn or had other dodgers tacked up over them.

Nevertheless Dutch had let his beard grow, and the mirror told him that he was unrecognizable except perhaps by close friends. He traveled to St. Louis without incident and put up at a cheap hotel near the levee.

His first act was to walk to the offices of the Baily-Keller Line. He stood across the street, smoking a cigar, and gazed at the building. What were his chances of getting past all the clerks to Baily's office? Probably very small. To see Baily he'd have to send his name in by one of a dozen clerks. And when Baily heard who was calling, he'd have Dutch searched.

That was no good. He walked along the street. What if he sent Baily a letter asking for a meeting somewhere? Then when Baily showed up he would plug him.

Well, no. Baily would certainly show up with hired body-guards.

What if he followed Baily home? Dutch had no idea where he lived, but it ought to be possible to tail him. He might get his best chance at Baily there—if he were patient.

That listened better. He paused at the corner and regarded the building. He would doubtless need a rifle for that kind of work, but a rifle was easy to get. With any luck at all, he could lay off and bushwhack Baily in his carriage. The idea made him smile.

He tossed away the stub of cigar. First things first. Baily would go home in a carriage, and they probably kept the vehi-cles around behind the building. He found an alley and walked down it, looking at the stables that lined it on both sides. Behind the Baily-Keller Building was a large yard with wag-ons and carts standing near a loading dock. In a long covered shed was a row of buggies and carriages and at the far end of roofed corral where the horses for these vehicles were kept.

But which carriage belonged to Baily?

It was disappointing that there had been no turning up of Dutch despite all the wanted dodgers that had been distributed.

Ki said, "If he goes out in public he probably changes his appearance. Maybe he grew a beard."

Jessie nodded. That would be the obvious thing to do. "Or perhaps he wears spectacles."

There had been no other steamboat robberies that were in any way like the ones Dutch had been responsible for since the one near Simcoe. The bandits had gotten a good haul there.

Jessie said, "I think they're somewhere spending it."

"Yes, probably. And there are only a million towns along the river."

"But not that many big cities. And we agreed a long time ago that he would head for a big town—like St. Louis or New Orleans."

Ki smiled. "Which one are you partial to?"

"New Orleans," she said at once, thinking of Denis Foucaud.

"It's as good a guess as any," Ki replied.

They were standing at the Grogan landing, looking at the cluster of fishing craft and small boats tied there.

"Let's get our bags packed," Ki said. "We can get the next boat south."

There were several handlers in the yard, but Dutch knew that if he asked for information, especially about Baily, he would be remembered. There was only one entrance and exit from the carriage yard, so he stationed himself in a nook of the building across the street, and waited.

Would Baily give him blackmail money when he asked for it? He was probably being foolish to think so. Baily might agree, then send toughs after him. That was Baily's way. Baily was just as much a criminal as he was, Dutch reflected. Now that he was here on the scene, and could be face to face with Baily within hours, he was less and less sure that the blackmail scheme was a good one. Baily would certainly want time to get the money together—and he'd use that time to see that he, Dutch, was eliminated from the earth.

And he would want Dutch eliminated because Dutch knew too much about his plans. The only sensible thing, Dutch thought, was to finish Baily. That way he would protect himself. Baily was the only one who could point a finger at him as the person who'd robbed the steamboats.

It was a two-hour wait until he was rewarded by sight of Johnson Baily as he walked from a rear door of the building, accompanied by another well-dressed man. The two halted and talked for several minutes, then Baily went toward the shed and out of Dutch's sight.

After a short wait, he reappeared sitting in a black carriage. He was the only occupant and was unfolding a newspaper as the rig passed Dutch. The driver sat on a high seat, wearing a top hat and a tightly buttoned overcoat.

Dutch jogged after the carriage, which moved slowly because of wagon traffic. It was easy to keep it in sight.

The carriage halted once near the edge of the business district, and the driver climbed down, conferred for a moment with Baily, then went into a shop. Dutch moved close to the carriage. Baily could not possibly spot him—unless he climbed half out of the coach. Dutch could see the monogram on the carriage door: JB in red, with curlicues.

When the driver returned with a package, he gave it to Baily and climbed back onto the seat. The carriage moved on. The streets were less crowded and the one-horse coach made better time. Dutch was forced to run to keep it in view.

And then, just when he had about decided he could no longer keep the top hat in sight, the carriage turned into a residential street, slowed and came to a halt.

Dutch stopped at the corner, panting hard. He watched Baily get out of the carriage and put the parcel under his arm. He walked up the steps to the house as the coach moved on. Dutch smiled. So this was where Baily lived.

He waited till Baily disappeared into the house; then he approached it and made certain he would know it again, a large two-story frame building painted brown, with two chimneys, set on a slight rise from the street, with several clumps of small trees in front. Lights were on in a number of the rooms, and Dutch wondered if Baily were married. It had not occurred to him before.

Looking at the sky, he decided it would be dark within the hour. He did not dare hang around the street; someone was sure to notice him and be able to describe him. He walked back the way he had come, for a mile or more, then turned and came back slowly. It was dark when he reached the house again and he went much closer.

There was a long drive, and he walked along it cautiously and came to a stable that faced an alley. The house had a wide yard with trees and a garden, a hedge and a tall fence along the alley. Moving close to the rear of the house, he could hear the sounds of someone in a kitchen. A cook was doubtless preparing supper.

He returned to the front of the house, trying to see in, but the windows were all draped. Swearing under his breath, Dutch crossed the street and stared at the brown house. There was no way he could fire into it and hit Baily. He'd have to wait until his victim came out.

Then he'd shoot him in the carriage.

The next day he bought a rifle, a used Winchester .44. With a pocket full of ammo, he hired a saddle horse from a livery and rode out of town. Away from houses, he selected a place to put up a target and paced off one hundred yards.

He fired five shots at the target, aiming carefully. He examined the target; the rifle was shooting slightly to the left. He corrected and fired again and was satisfied the shots would go where he wished.

The next thing was to decide where to ambush Baily.

That evening, still on the horse, he tailed the carriage again and saw that the driver followed the same route exactly.

There was one section along the route where there were fewer houses or buildings. He would wait there for Baily, step into the street when the carriage passed and shoot into the back of the vehicle. He was sure to hit Baily that way, and he'd get away on the horse.

And he'd do it the next evening.

★
Chapter 13

Lieutenant Denis Foucaud was delighted to see them when they arrived in New Orleans aboard the *Julia*. Jessie sent him a note immediately, and he rushed to the hotel and had dinner with them.

"What news of the chase?"

"Very little," Jessica replied. "We think Dutch's gang may be down to two members aside from himself—but we can't be positive." She told Denis about Karl Loder in Grogan. They were sure Karl had shot Cy, thinking he was Dutch. "Of course he admits nothing."

"And you two are here in New Orleans because you think Dutch may be here?"

Ki said, "It's possible. He has money to spend."

Denis shook his dark head. "There's not a smell of him. Not a nibble from all the posters we've put up—not counting the crazies who confess to all the murders on a regular basis."

Jessica sighed. "That's not good news."

"We think he's changed his appearance," Ki said hopefully. "He'd be a fool not to."

Denis shook his head again. "I have informants who could

turn up a blackbird on a coal barge at midnight. They swear to me that Dutch is not in this city."

"What about the jewelry they stole?"

Denis shrugged slightly. "I never had much hope of recovering any of that. It's all been broken up by now, melted down, the stones reset . . ." He smiled at Jessie. "It's also probably been sold and resold a dozen times too. You could be wearing some of it right and never know it."

She put a hand to her throat. "I hope not . . ."

The meal finished, Ki excused himself and left Jessie and Denis together. Jessie went with Denis into the main ballroom, where an orchestra was playing. They danced for more than an hour . . .

It was fun to be with him, holding hands and feeling his kiss on her cheek when the lights lowered during the numbers.

He whispered in her ear, "I've thought about you every day since you left here."

"And I thought about you too."

"It worries me that the man you're seeking is a killer."

"Yes, I know."

"What if he should turn on you?"

"I doubt he knows we're after him."

He brushed his lips across her cheek. "But you can't be sure of that. He might know more than you think."

"Maybe—but we take precautions. Ki is a tiger when danger approaches."

"I worry about you just the same."

It was very pleasant in his arms. And more than pleasant to think he cared. Before midnight they went up to her room and undressed by candlelight, sliding into bed together.

He said, "I think I should lock you up and never let you out of my sight again."

Jessie laughed. "In one of your jails?"

"No—in my heart."

She kissed him. "Let's talk about that when we lock up Dutch and his gang."

"You're never going to lock up Dutch."

"Oh? Why not?"

"Because I have a feeling he won't be taken alive."

77

She said philosophically, "That's a bridge we'll cross when we get to it."

He held her close. "All right—that's enough talk about Dutch."

She snuggled closer, "I agree . . ." She tightened her arms about him and he rolled her onto her back. She sighed deeply, with a feeling of great comfort and satisfaction, as she felt him enter her.

Across the room the candle flickered in the gloom, and a light rain pattered softly against the windows.

Johnson Baily had heard nothing from Hap Stoker for a week. Where the hell was the man? Baily hoped he was tracking down Dutch Rollins. He hadn't asked Stoker for regular reports, but he should have. It was annoying not to know.

In fact a number of things were annoying him. The stockholders were beginning to carp and complain about the running of the company. Why were profits down? He had even heard talk of replacing him. Of course they could not do it; they were frustrated.

He had prepared a letter detailing why the company was experiencing a low point. That would not last, he explained, and he hoped the stockholders believed him. The letter would be posted in a few days and would perhaps smooth over some of the soreheads.

In the afternoon he received a message from an actress he had met recently. She wanted to know if he would like to see her show. Enclosed was a ticket.

Baily smiled, thinking of her. He sent down for a supper and ate it in the office and later went downstairs for his carriage and was driven to the theater.

Dutch took his time loading the rifle, looking at each brass cartridge. Then he dressed warmly; it was turning cold outside. He got a horse from the stable and rode slowly to his selected position along the route of Baily's accustomed homeward journey. He arrived slightly more than a half hour early, and it was getting dark.

He got down and stamped his feet, looking at the sky. There

would be plenty of light to shoot by.

The half hour passed.

Then an hour passed and no carriage with Baily inside. Had they taken another route? Dutch was disgusted. He mounted the horse and rode to Baily's house. The usual lights were on inside, but they told him nothing.

He rode around to the alley and down it to Baily's stable. The doors were tightly closed, and he could not tell if the carriage was inside or not.

He gave it up and went back to the hotel.

Baily hugely enjoyed the theater presentation. It was a comedy and his actress friend was excellent, as he told her over a late supper. Her name was Dawn, and she cuddled up to him in bed in a nearby hotel.

He got home at three in the morning, exhausted and not entirely sober.

He was very late getting to the office next morning and complained all day long. Nothing pleased him. When he finally left, he felt drained. He wedged himself into a corner of the carriage and fell asleep, slowly sinking down till he lay on the seat, unmindful of the jolting ride.

He woke to a terrible smashing and pounding—rifle shots! He was in a field of fire! He rolled off the seat onto the floor of the carriage, screaming at Henry. He was being fired at! "Gallop the goddamn horse!"

For long moments his mind whirled with shock—who the hell was shooting at him? Someone wanted to rob him? He looked up to see the back of the carriage shredded where bullets had torn it. Somehow Henry, on his high seat, had survived—the sniper had not been shooting at him.

If Baily had been sitting in the seat as usual, he would now be dead! He took a long, deep breath. He could thank Dawn for that.

The shooting had stopped, but the horse was still galloping along the road and the carriage was swaying wildly. Never before had it been raced this way. Baily shouted to Henry to slow down as he clambered up to the seat again.

Looking back, he could see nothing in the gloom. The back

of the coach was a ruin. A fusillade of bullets had smashed it—right where his back would have been.

At Baily's house, Henry climbed down and looked in at him. "You all right, Mr. Baily?"

"I'm all right. Were you hit?"

"No sir . . ."

"You'd better go to the police. Tell them someone tried to rob us."

"Yes sir . . ." Henry opened the door and helped Baily out. Baily paused, looking both ways. From now on he'd go armed. Who the hell had shot at him?

Dutch had stood quietly by the horse as the carriage approached. He was on the side of the animal away from the approaching rig. He levered the rifle, putting a shell in the chamber. This should be easy.

It was dark and he could see no one in the carriage, but Baily had to be there, else the carriage would not be on the way home. He watched it rattle past him, then he stepped into the road and raised the rifle.

He fired eleven shots into the back, just where he knew the seat would be. By the time he got off eleven rounds, the coach was drawing away rapidly as the driver used his whip.

Dutch smiled. "Good-bye, Baily," he said aloud. He liked the sound of it and said it over and over again as he rode toward the hotel.

He tossed the rifle into a clump of brush and lit a cigar, feeling a considerable lift. Stopping at a saloon, he celebrated with half a dozen drinks, then staggered to the hotel and up to his room, where he fell across the bed fully dressed.

He had a miserable headache in the morning when he woke and went downstairs about noon. He had breakfast and several cups of coffee, which helped. Feeling better, he bought a newspaper at a street stand and went inside to sit in the lobby, looking for news of the shooting.

He found the item on an inside page. Someone had tried to kill Johnson Baily, president of the Baily-Keller Steamboat Line. Tried to kill? Dutch scowled at the paper. He had failed? How the hell could he have failed!

80

According to the police report, the bullets had missed Baily. How was that possible?

His name was not mentioned, Dutch saw with satisfaction. The item speculated that a robber had done the deed. Dutch sighed, took the paper up to his room and read it again. But it still said the same thing. Baily was unharmed.

After all his trouble.

★

Chapter 14

Jessica and Ki read the account of the Baily shooting as they returned to St. Louis on a steamboat. A boy had come aboard at Memphis and sold papers and fruit to passengers.

"Who would want to kill Baily?" Ki asked. "A robber maybe?"

"Possibly a random thing, as the paper suggests. A robber might have thought he'd carry large sums with him."

"It doesn't listen right." Ki shook his head. "This looks planned. The shooter met the carriage in a lonely spot. I think it was an assassination that didn't come off."

"A robber could plan it, couldn't he? The carriage driver states he saw a man with a horse by the side of the road."

"Well, this robber evidently waited for Baily and no one else." Ki shook his head again. "I don't like it. A robber would have stopped the carriage and had Baily get out. Instead, he fires into the back of the coach, obviously trying to kill Baily. He made no move to stop the carriage."

"Hmmmm. That's true."

"Could it have been Dutch?"

She looked at him in surprise. "Why would Dutch want to kill Baily?"

"I wish I knew. Maybe we'd better ask him what enemies he has."

"And we'd best talk to Sergeant Tyler."

"Yes. First thing."

Sergeant Tyler was happy to see them. "What did you learn in New Orleans?"

"Not a great deal," Jessie said, "unfortunately. The police swear that Dutch is not in their city."

They met in the same park as before and walked along the grass slowly. Tyler was in charge of the Baily shooting incident. He agreed with Ki that it certainly looked like an assassination attempt. "We haven't mentioned that possibility to the press," he told them. "We've let the reporters think we consider it a random affair. Maybe we won't scare off the shooter."

"Could it be Dutch?" Jessie asked.

The policeman's eyes rounded. "Dutch? I never considered him. Why would he shoot Mr. Baily?"

"We don't know."

Tyler said, "Right now Baily has a lot of disgruntled stockholders on his hands because of the poor condition of the company. One of them could have taken a shot at him. I've got men checking out that angle."

Ki said, "Then you haven't turned up anything about Dutch?"

"No. Not a thing."

They left Tyler, went to the Baily-Keller Building and talked to the foreman in charge of the carriage yard. He had big eager eyes for Jessica, and when she asked to speak to Baily's driver, he found the man for her at once. "His name's Henry Rasson."

Rasson was a heavy black man who bowed politely to her, lifting his hat. He had worked for Mr. Baily five years, he told them, and never had any trouble before.

She said, "The man you saw by the side of the road just before the shooting. Can you tell us what he looked like?"

Henry furrowed his forehead. "It was dark, missy. I didn't get a good look at him. Didn't know it would be important."

Ki offered, "You must have been a little surprised to see a man there in that particular spot at that time."

"Yes, sir, I was. But he didn't make no move to stop us . . ."

"Was there anything about him, anything at all you can remember?" Jessie persisted.

He looked at her, furrowing his forehead. "Well, no, missy. I don't remember nothin' . . . He had a beard and . . ."

"A beard!"

"Yes, a beard. Black hair."

"Was he a white man?"

"Yes, missy."

He had nothing else to tell them. They thanked him and when they left the yard, Ki said, "Dutch."

"But a lot of men wear beards. Thousands!"

Ki obtained one of the wanted posters and drew in a beard on Dutch's photograph. When he took it back to the yard and showed it to Henry, the driver said, "It could be him . . ."

One of Hap Stoker's many informants sent word to him that he was sure Dutch Rollins was in St. Louis, staying at the Hanover Hotel.

Stoker took the next available steamboat and arrived in that city three days later. He found that the Hanover was a cheap hotel not far from the waterfront and catered mostly to boat crews and workers, with a scattering of drummers and some older citizens.

He took a chair in a corner of the lobby and sat, watching people come and go. Several looked as if they might be Dutch—he had only the photograph to go by—and he followed them. The first man turned out to be a clerk in a hardware store. The second man he followed proved to be a mate on the steamboat *Atawanda*. The third went into the center of the city and sat down against a wall with a cup and pencils, begging.

Annoyed, Stoker returned to the hotel. It did not occur to him that Dutch might have grown a beard, so he did not give Dutch second glances when he went in and out.

Dutch went back to the Baily-Keller carriage yard but did not see Baily's usual carriage. It was probably in a shop somewhere, being repaired. He waited to see Baily, but he did not appear. After his close call, Baily was probably taking precautions, and Dutch could not discover what they were.

He hung around Baily's home, hoping to get in a shot, and saw him arrive several times with armed men. And then one night the police showed up and Dutch had to run. They chased him, but he managed to climb a high fence and elude them.

Baily was skittish as hell!

Dutch sat in a saloon with a beer in front of him. He would probably never be able now to plan ahead to get a bead on the man. Unless Baily settled down again—and that didn't seem likely in the near future. Whenever he managed to get a glimpse of Baily in public, Baily was always with one or two big men who had the look of bodyguards.

Dutch wondered if he might be wise to give up on Baily for the time being. His cash was getting low anyway. Maybe he should go back to Grogan and wait for the others to show up. When they got there, they'd be broke too of course. So they could all hit another steamboat and replenish their funds.

He sipped the beer. What they needed certainly was to find another safe, like the one on *Majesta*, with stacks of money in it. What a fool he'd been! He regretted over and over having given that fifteen thousand dollars back to Baily.

He left the saloon and moved along the levee, hands deep in his pockets. Now and then he noticed one of the wanted posters bearing his picture. But with the black beard he felt safe. His was an average-looking face anyway and with hair all over it, no one gave him a second glance.

He stopped and stared at a small steamer that was about to shove off, heading south. On a sudden urge, Dutch trotted across the levee and barely jumped on board ahead of the roustabouts pulling in the gangplank. He paid over his passage, saying he wanted to go to Natchez.

Standing on the boiler deck, he watched the steamer back out and head downstream. There was nothing in the hotel he wanted—another shirt. Let them have it.

It had been in all the papers that he lived and hung out in Grogan, so he suspected the police would keep an eye on the town. They might question everyone who got off a boat there.

He stayed in his stateroom as much as he could stand it and strode the decks at night, and when the steamboat approached Grogan, he was running in luck. It approached the town long after dark.

It was not a cold night, so Dutch wrapped his money in a bit of ground sheet, tied it tightly about his body, slipped over the rail when no one was about and dropped quietly into the water.

He was a strong swimmer, having spent his youth fishing and paddling the Mississippi. The water was chilly but not at all unbearable. He swam to the bank and climbed out, teeth chattering, and watched the steamboat's lights disappear in the distance. They would wonder what had happened to him.

He smiled at the lights of the town, a mile or so away. No one knew he was here.

He had landed downstream from the town, so he cut across the fields till he reached the road and turned south along it toward the house. Rudd and Aunt Mae were astonished to see him when he pounded on the door.

"Dutch! Where the hell you drop from?"

Dutch said, "I fell off a steamboat." He knelt by the fireplace and laid sticks on the coals.

Mae said, "You're all wet! Get those clothes off before you catch your death!"

Emory and Alley Trask had not yet shown up with the *Cynthy*, Uncle Rudd told him. "Was they comin' here?"

Dutch nodded. Maybe they had hit a winning streak and their money had lasted longer than usual. But then, it had only been about two weeks since they'd gone downstream.

As he sat on the rear steps next morning, watching old Rudd putter in the vegetable garden, Dutch thought about Karl Loder. He was convinced it had been Karl who had shot Cy. And he knew Karl would be keeping an eye out for him, but Dutch had to settle the score. If he did not, they would laugh behind his back in the saloon in town.

So that night he set out across the fields to where Karl lived. He could see no lights on in the house when he came near. Was Karl sitting in the dark, waiting for him? There was no way

86

Karl could know he was here. It didn't seem likely he would be waiting all this time . . .

Karl was no fool. He had friends who would keep him informed if Dutch got off a steamboat, and then he'd prepare. But no one had seen Dutch slip into the water and swim ashore; he was positive.

So why were there no lights on inside the house?

With infinite patience, Dutch crept to the outside wall of the house, put his ear to the siding and listened, hearing nothing. He reached up and felt the windows, all closed and locked. He crept to the front of the house, listening, smelling . . . The front door was tightly closed with a hasp and a big padlock on it.

Karl had gone somewhere. Damn!

He went around the house and found all the windows closed and locked. He bundled up his coat then and whacked it against a window, breaking the glass. Then he went into the barn, struck a match and rooted around for a kerosene tin. He found one half-full and took it back to the open window. He poured the oil inside, struck another match and dropped it over the sill.

The fire whooshed up instantly. Dutch walked back to the barn and watched the fire spread, crackling happily as it began to devour the house.

He walked into the fields then. People from surrounding houses would see the fire when it broke through the roof, and probably come to see what they could do, being neighbors. They'd be able to do nothing.

Dutch paused and looked back from a mile away. The glow lighted the sky a deep orange color.

In bed that night he stared at the dark ceiling. He had burned down Karl's house, but where was Karl? He still hadn't evened the score.

On the theory that it had been Dutch who had bushwhacked Johnson Baily, Sergeant Tyler deployed a squad of detectives. They visited every hotel in town, with the flyer of Dutch but with a beard sketched in.

In two days they struck pay dirt. A clerk at a cheap hotel near the levee, the Hanover, recognized the amended photograph.

"Yes, that man stayed with us—and he left a few things in his room."

"He isn't here now?"

"No."

"Is it possible he'll be back for his things?"

"I couldn't say. Maybe. It's happened before that one of our roomers gets drunk and forgets which hotel he lives at . . ." The clerk shrugged.

"Was he here alone?"

"As far's I know, yes. He was the only one in his room. It has a single bed."

Sergeant Tyler stationed a man at the hotel, in case. The rest of the squad went along the levee asking if this man— they showed the picture—had boarded a steamboat.

No one had noticed him.

It was like looking for a broom straw in a cornfield, Tyler said to Jessica and Ki. "I think he's left town. Took off in a hurry. Maybe he got news of something."

"He and the gang could be planning another robbery," Ki said.

Tyler agreed. "That's what I think.

Jessie asked, "Was he here with the others?"

"The clerk said he was alone."

"Then where are the others?"

"An interesting question," Tyler said. "Maybe Dutch came here alone to shoot Baily."

Jessie said, "I still don't understand why he would go out of his way to shoot Mr. Baily. Is there a connection between them we don't know about?"

"How could there be?" Tyler said in surprise. "Dutch is a small-time crook and Mr. Baily is a respected businessman. I doubt if they have ever even seen each other."

"Well, it's strange all the same," Jessie said.

"Let's get back to Dutch," Ki said. "Did he go to meet the others?"

"That's a good guess," Tyler agreed. "He could have gone downriver to Grogan. And if he did, we'll know it. We have an undercover man there. He'll wire us if Dutch gets off a boat."

● ● ●

The undercover man was Hank Summers, a policeman who had grown up on a fishing barge and who was at home with river rats and hangers-on.

He slipped into Grogan one night in a battered skiff and in hours was one with the footloose fraternity, not part of the town at all.

But he was in an excellent position to observe anyone who came off a steamboat, or any other boat for that matter, at the Grogan waterfront.

Dutch did not.

To send a wire, it was necessary for Summers to cross the river to the little town of Myra. He was ordered to report in every week—or whenever he had news of Dutch. His first reports were all the same: No news.

However, when Karl Loder's house burned down, he made a point of reporting it. It was a mysterious fire for one thing, and for a second, he and Dutch were enemies. It was said by many in the town that Dutch had started the fire or had a hand in it somehow, even though no one had seen him in town.

Sergeant Tyler wired him to do what he could to discover if Dutch were in Grogan secretly. It was possible he had gone there by means other than steamboat. After all, there were roads leading everywhere. It was also possible that someone else, a member of the gang perhaps, had set the fire.

Summers was ordered to listen to all the gossip and snoop.

He quickly learned about Rudd and Mae Rollins, the only surviving members of the family outside of Dutch, and where they lived. Summers went there at night and sidled up to a window.

Dutch was inside, big as life.

The next morning, Summers took the skiff across the river to Myra and wired Tyler. Dutch was in Grogan.

★

Chapter 15

Sergeant Tyler and his superiors had a plan drawn up, and set it in motion at once. Police officers from several jurisdictions would converge on Grogan and seal off the town and vicinity. They would then close in and arrest Dutch and anyone found with him.

To Tyler and the other police officials the plan seemed simple, direct and sufficient. Complicated plans with large forces were apt to go awry.

The plan was put into operation. Sixty policemen, in two groups, met near Grogan in secret and went over the map carefully, then took up their positions as required. It was a military operation and was carried out with precision.

The only thing it did not take into consideration was the fact that Dutch had been born in the town and knew every rock and tree within miles. When sixty city-footed strangers began to surround the Rollins farm, Dutch became aware that something unusual was happening.

He slipped out of the house. The police had taken up an extended line, five paces between men, and began to move in. Dutch slid into the undergrowth along a fold of ground and gained an arroyo, pushing himself into a brush-hidden cave.

The police passed him by, and he snaked out and slid down a slope into a wood, wondering who they were. Had Baily hired an army to attack him?

From a distance he heard someone hail the house, ordering him out.

He could not hear Rudd's reply. A shot was fired, and the men closed in about the house and barn. Dutch grinned. They would search the house and find nothing. Rudd would tell them some story or other, and that would be that.

He jogged along a forest path, heading south. He'd find a boat somewhere and go on to New Orleans to join Alley and Emory.

Sergeant Tyler had gone with the men from the St. Louis police force and participated in the surrounding of the Rollins house. They turned up nothing. Rudd Rollins swore that Dutch had not been there for a month.

However, Tyler talked with Hank Summers, who related in detail what he had done and seen. Dutch *had* been in the house. Tyler believed him. Somehow Dutch had eluded the men who had come for him. He had probably slipped out only minutes ahead of the police and had somehow gotten through their line. All the work and planning had gone up in smoke.

Wherever Dutch was, he was probably laughing at them.

Jessica and Ki were sorry to hear of the failure. Ki said, "We knew he was slippery . . ."

Jessie added, "Now, I think, we can be sure he set Karl Loder's house afire."

"Yes. It's one more crime to fasten onto him." Tyler studied them. "Where do you suppose he's gone?"

"You're sure he was alone in Grogan?"

"Our man swears he was. He *saw* Dutch in the house."

"Then he's gone to meet the others." Jessie smiled. "But that doesn't help much, does it? We don't know where the others are."

"Ummm," Tyler said.

When they returned to the hotel, a wire was waiting for Jessica. It was from Denis Foucaud in New Orleans. He had

91

heard from one of his informants that two of Dutch's gang were in the city, living high.

Ki asked, "How does he know they're Dutch's men?"

She folded the yellow paper. "Let's go ask him."

"A brilliant idea," Ki said gravely.

She smiled at him and put the wire in an envelope to send to Sergeant Tyler. She wrote out a note telling him where they were bound.

But before they left, Jessie called on Aunt Lydia in the rented house. Lydia was delighted to see her and was feeling very well indeed, she said. The terrible wound was getting better every day that passed, and irritating her less and less. The doctor came at regular intervals and changed the dressing. She was sitting in the sun and puttering about the garden, and longing more every day to return to her home in Memphis.

"The doctor says I will be well enough to go there in a few weeks if I wish."

"That's wonderful." Jessie kissed her cheek. "But Dutch and his men are still out there somewhere. You must stay here safe and secret until they're captured and jailed."

Lydia sighed deeply. "Oh, very well . . ."

They boarded the steamboat *Athena* and ran south, during the day, at the dizzying speed of twenty-five miles an hour. Several times they passed through gusts of light rain, and once they encountered a dense fog that required them to tie up to the bank until it finally lifted enough for the pilot to steer.

During the long, tiresome days on board, several young men flirted with Jessica, and she smiled at them, never allowing them too close. She was going to see Denis Foucaud in a matter of days!

But one of the men, on deck with her in late evening, attempted to force his attentions on her—as he thought, a helpless girl in a light summer dress. But he was astounded to find a pistol poking into his belly. Jessie asked him sweetly to leave and he did so hastily—and gave her a wide berth the rest of the journey.

Apparently he told the others what had occurred and they shunned her as well. Anyone who could handle a pistol that deftly was a she-cat and one to watch.

But New Orleans appeared at last, over the jackstaff, and the *Athena* nudged into a landing and disgorged her passengers and cargo. Ki signaled a hack, and they drove to a hotel, from where Jessie sent a note to Denis that they had arrived.

Denis was a long time getting to the hotel and apologized, saying he had been in a far corner of the city on police business and had not been able to get away at once. But he was overjoyed, as usual, to see Jessie . . . and Ki. They sat in an alcove of the barroom with a bottle of brandy nearby and talked.

Jessie and Ki told Denis of the attempt on Johnson Baily's life. Denis had seen the brief police report, but no details. He too wondered why Dutch would shoot Baily.

His eyes and ears, Denis said, had turned up two strangers to the city who called themselves in public by different names. But one of his informers, an attractive woman, had overheard them, in private, call each other Emory and Alley.

The police fact sheet on Dutch Rollins gave the names of the men suspected of running with him. Emory Boles and Alley Trask were two of them. There were two others, Lyman Yoder and Cy Carew, who were apparently not in New Orleans.

"We don't know about Yoder," Ki said, "but we know that Cy was shot in Grogan, probably by a man named Karl Loder."

"He's dead?"

"Very. You can cross him off your list."

Jessie asked, "Where are these two men now?"

"My people followed them to a house on Downer Street, and they're there now, at last report."

"Are you going to arrest them?"

Denis smiled. "I thought we'd wait to see if Dutch joins them. The house is well watched."

"Good. How long have they been in the house?"

"It's where they've been staying. They go in and out. The house is owned by a widow who lives elsewhere. She rents it out through an agent. Apparently the two have taken it for several weeks . . . or a month."

Jessie nodded. "It's safer for them than a hotel."

Denis smiled. "I'm sure that's what they think. They sleep there during the day and go out at night."

Ki said, "So the next move is for us to wait for Dutch?"

"Yes—or follow them if they leave." Denis shrugged lightly. "I think either Dutch will come here, or they'll go to meet him."

"That sounds logical," Ki agreed. "Where is Downer Street?"

"It's close to that gambling house, the Spotted Cat. That's probably the reason they took it."

Hap Stoker was frustrated. Locating Dutch Rollins was proving to be no easy task. Stoker knew something about criminals, how sly and cunning they could be, but Baily had assured him that Dutch was not much smarter than a swamp frog. He began to feel that Baily did not know what he was talking about. A man might not be a brain but still be devious as hell.

Stoker bought and read every newspaper he could get his hands on, hoping to find an item that would lead him to Dutch. There was an enterprising dealer in St. Louis who bought papers from towns up and down the river and sold them for good prices on the street.

But nothing turned up. Apparently the Dutch Rollins gang had temporarily gone out of business.

Then an informant told Stoker about the *Cynthy*. It was a small steamboat that had disappeared from the across-river trade and had turned up in the hands of several men, one of whom answered to the description of Dutch. Was it possible that Dutch and the gang had bought a steamboat?

Of course it was possible. Where was the boat now?

The informant did not know.

Stoker put out the word, up and down the river. Look for a small steamboat named *Cynthy*.

A week later he received a wire from a watcher. The boat *Cynthy* was tied up at the levee in New Orleans.

Stoker took the next boat south.

● ● ●

Dutch came upon a clump of houses near the riverbank, probably owned by farmers; he could see tilled fields in the gloom.
Farmers would probably be fishers as well. He hunted along
the riverbank for a boat and found three. One was larger than
the others, and he stepped into it quietly, finding the oars
neatly stowed. He cast off the line and shoved the boat out,
rowing into the current.

He let the river carry him.

Miles from the place he'd stolen the boat, he tied up to a
thick clump of trees that overhung the water and slept the
rest of the night. The next day, he went on, learning to steer
the boat with one oar while the river bore him along at a
good pace.

He ate all the food he'd brought, and that evening he steered
into the bank again when he glimpsed lights. Maybe he could
buy or steal some food . . . He tied the boat and walked inland
and, in a dozen yards or so, came to a road. The lights had
seemed near, but they were farther than he'd thought. He
came to a settlement—houses built with no particular pattern,
a deadfall, a store, some corrals and several barnlike buildings.
The settlement nestled in a curve of the river, quiet as a turtle
in a mud bank.

Except that when Dutch drew near, he could hear in the
saloon voices raised in song, wavering and doubtless whisky-
soaked.

He entered the store. It was a rectangular room with shelves
everywhere and various articles hanging from the ceiling and
walls. The place smelled of coffee and beer. In the center
of the room, there was a large black belly stove, around
which sat five men. They stared at Dutch, and conversation
halted.

Dutch nodded. "Howdy."

One of the men said, "You come off a boat?"

"Just come across the river," Dutch said. "Didn't know this
place was here."

Another man asked, "Come across from where?"

Dutch frowned at them. "I come across the goddamn river.
Who owns this here store?"

95

A man with a soiled apron about his middle got up. "I do. What you want?"

Dutch pointed to the glass case on a counter. "Take some of that cheese. You got any bread?"

"No more bread. But I got crackers."

"I take them. Take some airtights too, peaches if you got 'em."

"Got plenty."

A man at the belly stove asked, "Where's your boat?"

Dutch turned to face them, pressing his elbow against the Colt revolver under his coat. "It's down there a bit." He inclined his head south. "What you askin' all them goddamn questions for? I come across the river and I go back when I goddamn well feel like it."

Another man said, "Who you know across the river?"

Dutch was exasperated. He slammed money down on the counter and took the newspaper-wrapped parcel the store-keeper shoved toward him. As he walked toward the door a voice said loudly, "Just a minute."

Dutch glanced back. One of the men was standing. He drew a pistol. Instantly Dutch picked an apple from an open barrel by the door. He flung it at the man, drew his own revolver and fired two shots, one of which rang on the stove. He slammed out of the store and ran into the dark.

Shouts followed him, and someone fired through the closed door. He ran north along the dim road, hearing the men spill from the store. They were all shouting, and more lights appeared.

Dutch slowed to a trot, grinning. They would mill around until they finally listened to a leader. Then it would be too late. They would probably head south anyway.

He left the road and moved slowly along the riverbank till he came to the boat. No one was following him. He took time to reload the revolver, shoved it into his belt and pushed the boat off. He paddled into the darkness, and the current caught the boat in midstream, far out from the land. The shoreline was only a misty blur, and he knew no one could see him at all.

He slid by the settlement, still hearing a few shouts, which seemed very far away, then he left the lights behind. What had

96

gotten them so riled up? He had heard about people along the river making and selling illegal whisky. Maybe that's what it had been about. Maybe they thought he was a revenue man. Dutch shrugged. That was their problem.

He opened the parcel and began to eat the crackers and cheese.

★

Chapter 16

When they finally struggled back to the Downer Street house, they were weary and broke. It was three o'clock in a misty, cold morning. Emory had less than twenty dollars in his kick, and Alley had half that.

But they had enjoyed one whale of a time! It was easy come, easy go. They had come to town to spend the money, and they had done exactly that—all in a little less than four weeks.

Alley sat on the bed. "Why don't we go back to Grogan in the morning?"

Emory agreed. "As soon as we wake up."

Alley got up and examined the calendar on the wall. "We owe another month's rent tomorrow. And more for the busted furniture."

Emory had broken two chairs in a fit of anger one day. They were expensive chairs. He said, "If we slide out tonight, we don't have to pay nothing."

Alley grinned and got out his duffel bag.

Lieutenant Foucaud had men watching the Downer Street house around the clock. One man was on duty at all times. The department could not spare more, though Foucaud argued that the back door was not covered.

The man on duty when the two suspects arrived home at 3 A.M. was Jules Maser. He watched them go inside, and when he tried the front door a while later, it was securely locked. They were in for the rest of the night—as always. They were probably in for most of the next day also—as always.

Jules curled up across the street in a porch corner and dozed. In a short time he was asleep. And while he slept, Emory and Alley came out of the house by the front door and walked off in the direction of the levee.

When they got to the boat, they paid off the young man who had slept aboard, guarding it, and prepared to leave at first light. Alley got steam up, and when the sun poked cold but rosy fingers into the trees, he backed the *Cynthy* into the river and headed upstream toward Grogan, far off in the north.

Jules Maser was awake when his relief showed up on time. The two suspects were safely inside, he told the man. They had come home early in the morning and were doubtless sleeping it off. Jules went home to breakfast.

His relief, Francis Olman, passed on the job to his relief, Burt Sanders. The two suspects were still inside, he told Sanders.

Sanders told that to Lieutenant Foucaud when he came by. Foucaud looked at his watch. "Nobody stirring?"

"They haven't come out. I haven't seen anybody."

"How long have they been in there?"

"More than a day, I guess, Lieutenant. Usually we see somebody moving about by now."

Foucaud thought about the back door, and a terrible suspicion began to steal over him. He told Sanders, "Go around the back and try the door. See if you can get in without breaking anything."

"Yes, sir."

Foucaud went to the front door. He turned the knob and pushed, and the door opened. He swore under his breath and moved inside silently, listening. Nothing. He walked into the parlor and looked at a ticking clock, the only sound in a lonely house.

The two suspects were not on the premises, nor were their possessions. They had slipped out sometime during the night.

There was no way the watchers on duty could be blamed. If they had covered the back . . . Foucaud sighed. Where had the two men gone? Had they noticed the watch on the house and gone to ground somewhere else? It was an interesting question. But not an appealing one.

Dutch pulled the boat to shore two days later at a small town landing. A faded sign proclaimed the town's name: Oakton. He had eaten all the food and had no beverage save river water—which had no kick.

There were a dozen boats tied up or grounded at the landing. A few men and boys were working on several, painting bottoms. Dutch said, "Howdy," and walked into town, a mile or so away. It was getting on to dusk.

The town straggled along a single main street that curved with the land. One of the first things he saw, tacked to a wall, was a flyer headed by the word "REWARD!." It bore a picture of himself with a black beard sketched in. He stood a moment and swore softly, staring at it. Then, glancing around, he tore it down and crumpled it into a ball.

The general store was almost in the center of town, a large building with two lamps glowing outside the door. Dutch pulled his hat down and walked in—he had to have food—hands in his pockets, trying to look like a farmer who had just left his plow in the field.

There was another flyer tacked to the outside wall of the store, glaring at him as he went by. The goddamn things were everywhere!

A solitary customer, a woman, was in the store talking to the storekeeper, a spare man with gray hair. She was complaining that the soap she'd bought did not get her clothes clean. He was shrugging, saying he could do nothing about it.

When she finally left, frowning at Dutch, he said, shaking his head, "That woman complains about ever' damn thing she buys. I wish to God she'd move away."

Dutch grunted. He told the storekeeper what he needed, and the man piled the items on the counter . . . as a tall,

100

dour-looking man entered, cradling a shotgun.

Dutch turned, and the man pointed the double-barrel. "You won't be needin' them vittles," he said.

He had a silver star on his coat. Dutch gritted his teeth, knowing he would never be able to snake out the Colt before he had a large hole in his middle. A hole that could not be repaired.

Slowly he raised his hands.

It was not easy for Denis Foucaud to tell Jessica and Ki that the two, Alley and Emory, had slipped away in the night—and he had no idea where they had gone.

"I think they must have detected the watchers somehow and gone out the back door."

"Your men will find them," Jessie said encouragingly.

"I hope so. But if they're alerted, it won't be easy. We'll have to begin all over again."

Ki said, "We have to assume they went to meet Dutch. Or maybe Dutch came to the house . . ."

"I doubt that," Foucaud said, shaking his head. "That would mean letters or messages back and forth, and we know nothing of the sort was delivered to the house. I think it's likely they arranged a meeting place well ahead of time."

"Which could be anywhere . . ."

"Yes. I'm afraid so."

The tall deputy took Dutch to the local jail house, located near the end of town. It was a fieldstone building, backed into a slope of hill like a badger, with a log roof on which grass was growing. Dutch sighed deeply on seeing it.

The building had only two rooms—the front part was an office; the back was the barred jail. It had two dank-looking cells, and Dutch was put into one of them.

The cell contained a rickety iron cot, a slop bucket, one high-up window with bars and a stone floor. Dutch found a stub of candle under the cot, and when it got dark he struck a match. The candle might last an hour or two . . .

He spent a miserable night. It was cold, and the single blanket, over his clothes, did not warm him. In the morning

101

a boy showed up with a tray. It held a plate of food, a mug of coffee and a wooden spoon.

The boy was a cheerful sort who looked to be fifteen. "My name's Boyd. How you, Mr. Dutch?"

Dutch grunted. The lad shoved the tray under the bars.

"You get another'n this evenin'."

"Can I have a candle and another blanket?"

"I'll ask the deppity. You got smokes?"

Dutch's brows rose. "You bring me some cigars?"

"Sure. You got any money?"

Dutch handed over a dollar. "Get a candle too. Is there only one deputy in town?"

"Yeah. That's Mr. Rankin. He been deppity here since I remember. He kind of gruff, ain't he?"

"I seen more jolly."

Boyd laughed. "He that way all through too. Nobody ever seen that man laugh. You best eat them beans afore they gets cold."

The boy left, and Dutch finished the food and the bitter coffee in the white mug. Then he lay on the cot and stared at the gloomy ceiling. What would happen next? Probably Deputy Rankin would wire someone to come and get the prisoner. They'd take him to some big town like St. Louis and try him. They'd convict him and Rankin would get the reward. Dutch grunted. Then Rankin would laugh.

He squirmed uncomfortably. That was no good, going on trial. It would take them no time at all to call him guilty. Sure as a gun. He'd either hang, or they'd shove him into some far-off prison for the rest of his life, probably at hard labor.

It was those damned posters that had done it. The deputy must have seen him—he probably watched all strangers—when he walked into town. A sharp-eyed old coot and his goddamn shotgun, probably eager to use it.

What would Alley and Emory do now? When they shot their wad in New Orleans, they'd go back to Grogan, looking to meet him. He hoped they'd have sense enough to stay out of sight.

How in hell would he get out of this jail?

Boyd returned just before it got dark. He had another tray and more coffee. This time the food was grits, with some hard biscuits.

The boy said, "Your cigars is on top, Mr. Dutch." He shoved the tray under the bars. "They's a candle there too."

"Thanks." Dutch laid the cigars on the cot. "Where's the deputy?"

"He gone over to Elger, to the telegraph. We ain't got one in town."

"Where's that?"

"It's a long way. 'Crost the river and over east a piece. Maybe a hunnerd miles. He be gone a day'r two."

Dutch put the tray on his knees as he sat on the cot. "There's no law in town?"

"We don't hardly need no law here." Boyd held up a key ring. "I got the jail keys now. Guess I'm the law." He grinned, shaking them.

Dutch paused, the spoon halfway to his mouth. "What'll you take f'them keys, kid?"

"Oh Jezis, Mr. Dutch. I couldn't do that."

"How about a hunnerd dollars?"

The lad's eyes grew round and he took a quick breath. Dutch knew he had never seen that much money in his life. But he slowly shook his head.

"They'd know, Mr. Dutch. They ain't any way they wouldn't know."

"Two hunnerd dollars, kid."

Boyd backed away, then ran out and slammed the door. Dutch gave a great sigh. Too much temptation. He swore and picked at the food.

★

Chapter 17

Deputy Rankin did not return for nearly eight days. And Dutch did not see Boyd during that time. An older man came in with the trays and took them away, but he would not talk to Dutch. At every question, he shook his head. Once, he pointed to his ears and Dutch supposed him deaf. He did not respond no matter what Dutch said to him.

Rankin came into the cell room and said gruffly that men would be coming for him soon.

"Where they going to take me?"

"St. Louie, I figger. Put you on trial there."

"Then you get the reward?"

Rankin's eyes glittered for a moment. "That's right." He went out and left Dutch growling to himself.

After Rankin had returned, Boyd came in again with the trays. The first several times he did not stop to chat. Dutch said he was sorry he'd tempted him that way, and Boyd nodded and made a face.

Then Dutch said, "I give you two hunnerd dollars for a pistol."

Boyd stared at him. "A pistol!"

"A revolver, kid. Loaded. You can bring it in with a tray.

Nobody'd ever know. If they take me again, I'll tell 'em I had it hid."

He saw Boyd lick his lips. The boy wanted that money. Bad. "You won't shoot your way out of here?"

"Hell no. I use it on the boat after they come and get me. Miles from here."

"Three hunnerd."

Dutch hesitated. "All right. Three hunnerd. But git me a good gun and some ca'tridges."

Boyd nodded and went out.

Dutch smiled at his back. There was little possibility of him using the gun on the boat. They'd search him good before they took him out of the jail. He'd have to use it on Rankin.

That evening when he brought in the tray, Boyd also had a Smith & Wesson revolver under his shirt. He passed it and a handful of brass through the bars silently, and Dutch counted out three hundred dollars.

The gun was a nickel-plated double-action piece with most of the plating gone. Dutch smiled grimly and tucked it into his belt.

Alley Trask and Emory chugged upriver in the *Cynthy*, going slowly because they were beginners; they followed other boats when possible, because neither of them knew anything about river channels. Three times they ran aground on sand bars, not knowing how to watch for them. Luckily they were able to back the shallow draft boat off each time.

When they reached the vicinity of Grogan, they nudged the boat into the bank, concealing it under overhanging tree branches in a bit of cove. It was a lonely spot, and the surrounding area seemed as untouched by man as the day the world had been created. The country near Grogan was sparsely settled at best.

They had to leave the boat unguarded; there was no help for it. There was no point in leaving one of them behind since one man could not operate the boat alone. They trudged overland to reach the road south of town and piled rocks off to one side to mark the spot, so they could find the boat again.

No one was on the road; they turned in at the Rollins house

late in the afternoon. Aunt Mae was sitting on the porch, wide-eyed at seeing them. "Well, my land! Where you two been?"

"Down to New Orleans. Is Dutch here?"

"No. We ain't seen him for a spell."

Rudd came around the house, a rake in his hand. "Is Dutch comin' to meet y'all?"

"Yes. We figgered he'd be here now."

"Well then, he'll turn up. One o'you boys bring in some wood for the stove and we'll fix supper early."

Dutch waited for his opportunity. He had no idea how long it would take law officers to come to Oakton. Probably not too long, a matter of a week or so. And if they took him to a big city like St. Louis, he was through. A big town would have a big, strong jail.

He had to do it here.

Now that the deputy was back, Boyd had no keys. Rankin wore them on his belt, but Rankin seldom came into the jail area. The door to the office was kept closed, but Dutch could see the line of light under the door when Boyd had picked up the evening tray and departed for the night. Now and then he could also hear small sounds, a chair scraping on the floor . . . someone coughing . . .

Rankin must be out there in the office.

Dutch examined his newly bought revolver. He ejected the brass and looked at each round critically, then reloaded the weapon and shoved it into his belt, hidden by his coat. Then he began to yell and kick the bars.

He kept it up for five or six minutes, but it brought no response. Swearing, he picked up the iron cot and slammed it against the bars, over and over again. It made a terrible racket.

And it brought Rankin to the door. He growled at Dutch, "What the hell you doin'?"

Dutch continued to yell, ignoring the deputy, and Rankin strode to the bars, his face contorted. "Stop that goddamn caterwaulin'!"

Dutch took a quick step, reached through the bars and

106

grabbed Rankin's shirtfront. At the same instant, he pulled the pistol. As Rankin shouted and fought to get free, Dutch shot him three times in the chest and belly.

Rankin dropped to the floor and sprawled limply onto his face, dead before he fell. Dutch hauled the body close, unfastened the belt and got the key ring. He tried several keys in the lock before he got the right one. The door opened and he dragged the body inside.

There were splotches of blood on the floor. He went into the office. In the desk he found a Colt revolver and the shotgun standing in a rack. The Colt was a better gun than the pistol he'd bought from Boyd. He tossed the Smith into the drawer and shoved the Colt into his belt.

There was ammo in the desk, and he filled his coat pockets, took the shotgun and doused the office lantern. He looked out at the street; no one was stirring. Probably nobody had heard the shots in the jail. The walls were too thick.

He could see a few lights on in the town, but no one was in the street. Probably most people here went to bed with the chickens. What was there to do in a little burg like Oakton?

Dutch walked along the unlighted street toward the river, alert for any sound. There were several wagons parked on the street, and as he went by one near an alley, he could hear voices muttering. A few men were talking quietly in the shadows.

He saw no one else and gained the waterfront without incident. It was dark and deserted. Probably a big riverboat tied up at Oakton once in a generation. The boat he had stolen was pulled up on the bank, out of the water. He examined the others and selected one, a dinghy with oars in the bottom. He stepped into it gingerly, deposited the shotgun and blanket and cut the painter with his knife.

He pushed out with an oar and settled himself. As he rowed away from the landing, the current caught him and he smiled. He had made it.

It was cold in midstream. He pulled the blanket about his shoulders and hunched down. He was free—but he was going in the wrong direction. He wanted to go upstream. Grogan was probably a hundred or more river miles away. He decided to go across the river and wait at a wood yard or a landing for a steamer. He touched the beard. Damn! His face was on every flat surface, it seemed. It was probably on every steamboat too.

Maybe he had better go by land. Steal a horse.

It would take longer to get to Grogan that way, but he'd have a better chance of arriving in one piece and without leg irons.

The news that Dutch had been caught and was incarcerated in a little one-horse town called Oakton, was flashed up and down the river. A small-town deputy had recognized Dutch as he walked into town to buy victuals. The deputy had put a shotgun on Dutch and marched him òff to jail.

Jessica and Ki read the account in a New Orleans paper, and soon after Denis Foucaud called on them at the hotel, his face wreathed in smiles. "They've caught him!"

Jessie asked, "Where will they take him for trial?"

"Probably to St. Louis. The best witness is there—your aunt. She'll testify and it will all be over but the hanging."

"I think we should go there and be with her." Jessie looked at Ki, who nodded.

Denis insisted they stay long enough to celebrate with dinner that evening. "We'll toast Dutch's entrance into a very hot place, namely Hell."

Ki studied the newspaper. "Nothing is said about the others. Apparently Dutch was alone."

"Maybe he was on his way to meet them when he was caught."

"Where is Oakton anyway?"

Denis shrugged. "A little town in the middle of nowhere. What about dinner?"

"Of course we'll join you." Jessie nudged Ki.

"With pleasure," Ki said gravely.

Hap Stoker read the account, wadded up the paper in disgust and threw it across the room. Some little hick lawman in a two-bit town was going to collect the reward! Son of a bitch! After all his work!

He was in New Orleans but had found no sign of the boat *Cynthy*. He had tacked up ads on the various bulletin boards near the waterfront, and a young man had responded, saying he had been hired to look after that boat for a week or two while the two owners were on business in the city.

He described the owners, and Hap jotted down the particulars. Neither of them was Dutch. The young man had names, but Hap was sure those were false. And the young man had no idea where the boat had gone. No one had mentioned a destination to him, and he had not stayed around to see the boat leave, but it had probably gone upstream.

That was not much help. Everything was upstream from New Orleans.

Hap could do nothing more about finding Dutch. Obviously he had not been in New Orleans at all. Was the gang breaking up? Stoker took the next boat north.

Johnson Baily read the accounts of Dutch's capture, and his forehead furrowed. It was very bad news. Why in hell hadn't Dutch put up a fight and been shot down! Nothing went right where Dutch was concerned. If they put him on the witness stand in court, he was sure to tell all he knew—that he had robbed steamboats on orders from him, Baily.

It was a charge that Dutch might never make stick, but it was an annoyance just the same. He'd have to defend himself—and it might start certain people thinking the wrong thoughts.

Why the hell hadn't Hap Stoker found Dutch instead of some hayseed deputy? Did anything ever work out for the best? And where was Stoker anyhow? He hadn't heard a report from the man for weeks.

He put the paper down. Would they bring Dutch here to St. Louis? The reporter thought they would. Baily scratched his chin. Was there any chance that Dutch might become deceased in jail? It was an idea that made him sigh deeply. Probably not. How he regretted ever employing Dutch in the first place! Nothing but trouble had stemmed from it.

• • •

It was a very pleasant dinner. Ki had excused himself, immediately it was finished, saying he had important things to take care of, leaving Jessie and Denis together.

Denis was sad, saying he hated to see Jessie leave. "You come in and go out of my life too quickly. And I cannot follow you—they tie me to the job in this place."

"I must go, my darling. But I will be back. When Dutch Rollins, the killer, is convicted, our job will be done, and then we will have all the time we wish."

"What about the others of the gang?"

Jessie shrugged lightly. "The police will take care of them. We swore to see Dutch convicted—and if that includes the others, so be it. At any rate, when Dutch is in jail, the others will probably not long survive."

"Let's hope not."

She touched his hand. "I have a bottle of unopened brandy in my room. I should like your opinion of it . . ."

He nodded thoughtfully. "I am an excellent judge of brandy. You have luckily come to the right person."

"I was sure of it."

She rose and they went upstairs.

★

Chapter 18

It was full dark when Dutch rowed to the opposite shore and pulled the boat up out of the water on a grassy slope. He rolled in his blankets beside it and managed to sleep fitfully till dawn.

At first light, he was up and tugged the boat into the trees, then cut branches to conceal it, in order to leave as dim a trail as possible.

That done, he took the rolled-up blankets under his arm, and with the shotgun on his shoulder, he set out, walking north along the river. He was in a densely wooded area at first, but then the trees thinned and he was able to see a distant house or two, far back from the river, where men worked in the fields. Occasionally he came across fishing boats tied to trees, waiting for their owners. He kept an eye out for horses but saw none.

He walked all day long. At midday he came to a rutted road that paralleled the river, and he followed it gratefully. It made walking easier than pushing through brush and tall grass.

The road took him to the little town of Wender. He approached it near dark, and when he saw the buildings, he sat down to wait for nightfall.

He entered the town cautiously, watching for people like Deputy Rankin, but he saw none. There were wagons and a few horses on the street but no people at all. He saw no posters either, a pleasant surprise. Of course it was a tiny burg, probably not more than a few hundred souls, he guessed. Those lawmen who plastered the wanted dodgers over the landscape might well have decided Wender was too small to bother with.

The town comprised only five stores, a livery barn and some corrals. As Dutch entered, the general store owner was about to lock up for the night. Dutch slipped inside the door, saying he had just come across the river, was traveling east and needed a few supplies. He looked for recognition on the face of the man and saw none.

The store owner was glad of the business and put the items Dutch asked for on the counter, then into a sack as Dutch counted out the money.

Dutch said, "D'you know anyone who might sell me a horse?"

"Saddle horse? Why yes. Old Jake was in here only yesterday saying he had horses for sale." The store owner walked with Dutch to the door and pointed to the dim road that wended its way eastward. "You go down thataway for 'bout a half mile, till you see a barn on your left that's about covered with vines. That's Jake's place."

Dutch thanked the man and slung the sack over his shoulder. It was a long half mile. The vine-covered barn was in a field with a worn fence around it. Inside the fence were cribs and a few trees and a near-round corral where five good-looking horses watched him approach.

Old Jake was in a back room of the barn. He came out at Dutch's hail, pulling on an old coat. "Whatchoo want?"

Dutch said, "Store owner said you might have a horse to sell. And a saddle too."

"Hell, got five good hosses. You look 'em over in the corral there." He began to unhook a lantern, then halted. "You got to have a hoss tonight? You mus' be in a terrible hurry, friend."

Dutch shook his head. "I c'n wait for daylight. You let me bed down in one o'your stalls?"

"Sure. Take any of 'em." Jake waved and went back to the room and bed.

In the morning, Jake made a breakfast of eggs and beans and invited Dutch to share them. Then they went out to the corral and Dutch leaned on the top pole, his eye taken at once by a young sorrel. Old Jake threw a rope on the horse and they talked a deal.

Jake threw in a bridle and asked a nominal charge for a used saddle and blanket. Dutch was mounted and on his way within the hour.

The river road, according to Jake, would take him for about twenty miles before it abruptly turned eastward. He could then go across country for another half dozen or ten, till he came to Argyle, a town about the size of Wender.

After that, Jake became vague. "I ain't been thataway for maybe thirty year, and things is like to change in that time."

Jake had honored the route by the word "road." It was really only a rutted, single-track pathway that had probably never seen a wagon or cart. It wandered back and forth as if laid out by a drunken pilgrim but generally kept the river in view.

Dutch let the horse take it easy, and it was late afternoon before he reached the place the road turned eastward and lost itself in the trees. It was probably another half day's ride to Argyle, so Dutch got down and made camp. He had not seen anyone all day, except for the distant boats on the river.

He made a tiny fire and broiled strips of the meat he'd bought, then curled in the blankets while the sorrel cropped grass.

The news that Deputy Rankin had been found shot to death in Dutch Rollins's cell in Oakton was flashed by telegraph to the world. A steamboat had been hailed from the Oakton landing and the news taken to the next town that boasted a wire. A search was then organized for Dutch.

Jessica and Ki, in their hotel in St. Louis, read the news item with some disgust. How had Dutch managed to get a gun while in jail? The newspaper speculated that it had to have been someone in the gang or someone on the outside who had passed the gun to him.

The body had been found by a young man who was described as a helper around the jail. He had come into the jail building in the morning and found the body and the jail door standing open. Dutch was missing.

The newspaper made much of the mystery. Who had given Dutch the gun? Or had someone else come into the jail and shot the deputy?

Jessie and Ki had a meeting with Sergeant Tyler in the little park. Tyler was of the opinion that the jail "helper" might be the one to question. It had to be someone on the outside who had supplied the gun.

"The deputy was a man of long experience," Tyler said, "even though he was stationed in a little one-horse burg like Oakton. He would certainly have searched Dutch carefully, and he wouldn't have missed an article as bulky as a pistol."

"That makes good sense," Ki agreed. "You're probably right about the jail helper."

Tyler nodded. "Dutch probably paid him a good sum for the pistol."

In the days that followed, Tyler received information about the search and the investigation. Men were looking through all the towns up and down the river near Oakton. A boat was missing from the landing, and it was speculated that Dutch might have gone down the river, the quickest course, or across it. He might even have doubled back to the Oakton side and headed west.

Various lawmen were interviewed by eager reporters, and all stated they had too few men to cover the long distances involved in the search.

Then the team at Oakton got a confession. The young man–jail helper confessed. His name was Boyd Edwards, and he told them, through tears, that he had sold a gun to Dutch for three hundred dollars. Dutch had promised him that he would not use the gun on Rankin.

Tyler said, "The kid was a fool to believe a man like Dutch. He prob'ly never had anybody but drunks to deal with. Now he's ruined his life . . ."

• • •

The next day, Dutch reached the little river town of Argyle at noon. It was a town about the size of Oakton. He camped outside, in sight of the rooftops, and waited for dark. At dusk he left the horse behind and walked into town. He wanted a place to buy scissors, but every store was closed and locked; even the two saloons seemed dead, though there was light coming from the doors.

He stopped in front of the dry goods store. It was the most likely to sell scissors. He wondered if the owner lived in rooms behind the store . . . But when he went around the building, he could see no evidence of this. The store had a back door and a single window, square and grimy.

Behind the several stores was a line of privies and some trash bins. He looked in all the privies. No one. He went back to the window, took off his coat and wadded it up. Holding it against the window, he pushed hard.

The glass broke, tinkling on the floor inside. He waited, perfectly still for several minutes, but no one came to investigate.

He lifted out shards of glass and cleaned the sill, then climbed in and dropped to the floor. The room was dark and smelled of tobacco. Scratching a match, he saw he was in a small office. There were two desks, pushed back to back, and he quickly found a pair of scissors in one. In the store, he found a display of small mirrors and put one in his coat pocket.

The back door was barred; he lifted the bar and opened the door. He walked back to the picketed horse, rode around the town and went on, following a river road north.

In the morning, he set the stolen mirror in the crotch of a tree and carefully cut off his beard and mustache, as close to the skin as possible.

Five days later he reached Grogan.

Emory and Alley Trask were flat broke after they gave their remaining money to Aunt Mae. They walked out in the fields, out of earshot of the house, to discuss their problem.

Should they wait for Dutch?

115

Alley said, "We don't know where the hell he is. With the search goin' on, he could be holed up somewheres and not about to show his face."

"Maybe he went back to New Orleans."

"And we can't stay here very long. They'll be lookin' here for Dutch. We ought to leave today."

"We got to have money," Emory said moodily. "It takes money to run the boat . . ."

"Then we don't wait for Dutch. We'll find us a steamboat—"

"You figger the two of us can handle it?"

Alley nodded. "Have to. We got no choice. What you say?"

"Guess so. But what about Dutch?"

"We can leave word with Rudd. If Dutch shows up, Rudd can tell him we'll meet him at Stander's place. What about that?"

Emory nodded approval. Stander ran a saloon in a little burg south of Cairo.

Rudd asked no questions when they told him they were leaving, and he promised to deliver the message to Dutch.

They fired up the boiler and took the *Cynthy* downstream. The nearest wood yard was ten or fifteen miles away on the far shore. They ran past the yard and turned into the broad stream below it. It was deep enough for the boat, for half a mile; they tied up out of sight of river traffic.

It was a lonely spot with no sign of a road. The area was heavily wooded, with thick underbrush. There were a few deer trails, but no manmade paths.

It was an ideal spot. A good omen, Alley said.

They made their way on foot back to a spot within sight of the wood yard. There was a small shacky house near the landing, with smoke rising from a pipe chimney. Cords of cut wood were piled high near the water, and someone was ryhthmically chopping on the far side of the house.

"How many's there?" Alley asked.

"Maybe two . . ."

But they saw no one until, after several hours of waiting, a steamboat appeared and came into the landing, puffing steam.

Then the woodhawk came out of the house. He was a big man with a checked shirt and a black beard. He and the mate conferred, then the boat's roustabouts set to work loading wood.

Alley wanted to rush aboard, but Emory pointed to the upper deck. Three rough-looking, heavily armed men had emerged from a cabin and were leaning on the guards, watching the loading.

When the loading was finished, the mate paid the woodhawk and the boat moved into the stream.

Alley gazed after the departing boat. "I hope they ain't got them on all the boats . . ."

"Prob'ly not."

Alley grunted. It was a hard enough life without armed guards on boats.

★

Chapter 19

Twice more, before dark, Alley and Emory watched steamboats load up on wood and depart. Neither boat had armed
guards aboard—that they saw.

As night fell, they moved in close. Someone had been
chopping wood, but he had disappeared. Only the woodhawk
remained in his house. They confronted him with cocked
pistols. He swore at them, but they tied his hands and feet
to a chair and, when he would not shut up, gagged him.

The first steamer to tie up after dark was the *Cleo*, bound
for Cincinnati on the Ohio. Emory and Alley waited till the
roustabouts from the steamboat swarmed around the cords of
wood under the basket lights. No armed men appeared on the
boat. Then Alley fired into the air, scattering the men.

Emory, with a gunnysack, demanded valuables from the
crew and passengers while Alley stood by him with a pistol
in each hand. All went smoothly until one of the well-dressed
older passengers objected violently to Emory's grabbing his
watch and chain. Alley swiped at him with the barrel of a
revolver, knocking him down, as the wound spurted blood.
Suddenly several other men surged forward, one drawing a
gun.

Alley fired into them, and three men went down heavily, writhing on the deck. Alley yelled at Emory, and the two backed to the gangplank as the crowd seethed and someone fired a gun from an upper deck.

Others in the crowd drew revolvers, and Emory fired into them; then he and Alley ran into the dark as bullets cracked by, rapping into trees.

But no one followed them into the woods. They fought their way back through brush and second-growth trees to the *Cynthy*. Alley complained of a stinging sensation in his side. When they lighted a lantern, they discovered that a bullet had scraped past him, leaving a bloody smear.

But they had several hundred dollars in cash and a good assortment of rings, stickpins and other jewelry. These would have to wait until they returned to New Orleans.

In the morning, they eased the boat into the Mississippi. They tied her in the same out-of-the-way spot near Grogan.

When they trudged over the fields to the Rollins house, Dutch was there.

At Cairo, the captain of the *Cleo* detailed the robbery-murders to the police. Four men and one teenage girl had died from the robbers' bullets. Nine persons were wounded and in the hospital. Two men were responsible, and their descriptions matched those of Alley Trask and Emory Boles, men who ran with Dutch Rollins.

Also, five witnesses had heard one of the two call the other Emory.

Dutch had not been with them, and the police speculated that he had not yet rejoined them. The two must have acted on their own.

The search was widened to include Alley Trask and Emory. Both were now listed as killers along with Dutch.

Jessica and Ki read the accounts glumly. The two men who had evaded the New Orleans police had shown up once more in their old roles. And this time they had committed five murders and wounded more.

Eyewitnesses, according to the papers, had stated that the two had panicked and fired wildly into the crowd. It was a

119

miracle more people had not been killed.

"All the searchers," said Sergeant Tyler, "have been warned to take no chances with any of the three, but to shoot to kill."

"Then we won't be able to question them," Jessie said.

"We'll take the bad with the good. At least if they're dead, they're out of the steamboat robbing trade—or any other trade."

Jessie said, "They might meet at Grogan. It's possible Dutch might go there—from habit if nothing else. He has relatives there."

Tyler merely grunted.

When they left the sergeant, Ki said, "Certainly the police will think of looking in Grogan . . ."

"The police are stretched very thin. After all, they have the towns and cities to protect. How many men can they throw into this search?"

"Yes, that's all true." Ki shrugged. "All right, let's go there—but to look and listen. I think the more questions we ask, the less we'll learn."

Jessie smiled. "Of course."

They bought passage on the steamboat *Julia* and left her miles above Grogan, telling the captain they were heading west. It was not uncommon for people to get off a boat in the middle of nowhere.

When the steamboat continued downstream, they walked along the bank looking for a small boat or canoe. Instead they found a raft. "This will do," Ki said, "for a short journey . . ."

It was large enough for two, and they floated downstream at night, pulling to shore when they saw the lights of Grogan in the distance. They dragged the raft out of the water—they might need it again—and spent the rest of the night waiting. The town would be locked up tight at that hour.

As dawn approached, they walked into the town and sat on a bench in front of the hotel. When a clerk opened the door, they told him they'd just gotten off a steamboat, and then they signed for rooms. They could see the curiosity in the clerk's eyes—probably very few got off boats at the Grogan landing.

120

Ki told him, "We'll rest up a bit, then go on westward in a day or two."

That afternoon, they hired horses from the livery, asking the man where they would find a pleasant place to ride, to pass the time. He sent them north of the town.

It was necessary then to make a wide swing, when they had left the town behind, to come up to the Rollins's house from the south. It took hours, and when they arrived they picketed the horses in a clump of trees and slipped along a deep arroyo to halt less than two hundred yards from the rear of the house, where someone was hoeing a garden.

Ki looked at the man through binoculars. "It must be Rudd." He passed the glasses to Jessie.

"No one else would hoe his garden," she agreed.

They waited. Once a woman came to the door and threw out a pan of dishwater, but nothing else happened. As the light faded, the man put the hoe away and went into the house.

Ki said, "If Dutch is there, would he stay in the house all day?"

"I doubt it," Jessie replied. "From what we know, he's a restless type."

Later they moved close to the house and looked in the windows. Rudd and his wife were sitting at a kitchen table, but no one else was with them and the rest of the house was dark.

"Dutch is not in Grogan," Ki said, and they rode back into town.

Johnson Baily was delighted to read in the local newspaper that the police had been warned about Dutch. He was considered armed and dangerous, and their admonition was to take no chances with him; the local chief said, "Shoot to kill! The man and his gang are vicious criminals. Save the court the trouble of trying them."

Dutch was only one of Baily's problems. He was in constant hot water with his stockholders who wanted to force him out of office . . . but could not. They questioned his leadership but could not muster the votes, because Baily held the majority.

But of course the financial statement of the last month was much improved—which helped in one sense and hurt in another. It helped Baily mollify the stockholders, but it hurt his agreement with Elliot Scully.

It helped because neither Dutch and his gang nor anyone else had been robbing Baily-Keller steamboats.

However, his binding agreement with Scully was in jeopardy. As soon as Scully came home from Europe, he would demand an accounting. Baily would have to say the line was prospering. Bad news.

He, Baily, would have to remedy that, and soon.

He hated to put himself into the hands of another crook like Dutch—but did he have a choice? Well, yes, he had one impossible choice. He could do the job himself. But if he did, he would probably bungle it. He was not a holdup man, and he doubted if he had the nerve. And to board a steamboat with a pistol in each hand was not the way to find out.

No, he had to hire someone. But who?

He thought about all the businessmen he knew. Which one was the most likely to have had dealings with shady characters?

Himself.

Baily swore and lighted a cigar to puff at the ceiling of his office. No one knew of his dealings with Dutch, and very few of his connection with Hap Stoker. He drummed his fingers on a chair arm. Stoker was a man who ought to be able to help him. But did he want Stoker to become more involved? He would probably not be able to control Stoker any more than he had Dutch.

No, what he needed was a man who was part killer and part weasel—and would do what he was told and keep his mouth shut. He needed someone who would be able to finish what Dutch had started—bring down the Baily-Keller Line and ruin it completely.

So Elliot Scully could buy it for ten cents on the dollar.

★

Chapter 20

Jessica and Ki did their best to make themselves inconspicuous in Grogan, but it was not an easy task. Men stared at Jessie, licked their lips and went into the saloons to talk about the honey-blonde with the sea-green eyes and the great tits.

None of this was lost on Ki. "Let's take advantage of it."

"What do you mean?"

"Dutch could show up at any moment—he and the gang have a boat, after all. And they don't have to come here, through the town."

"Yes . . ."

"So we should watch the Rollins house."

"What are you getting at?"

Ki smiled. "I suggest that you stay here and make yourself visible while I go keep an eye on the house."

"Ahhhh, I see. But that's not exactly a division of the work."

"Well, we do what we do best. Very well, I'll stay here and make eyes at the men and you go and watch the house."

She laughed. "All right, you win. Go and watch the house. I'll sit and read the newspapers."

"Where everyone can see you."

"Yes. As you say."

"If anyone asks about me, I'm upstairs sleeping." He knew no one would ask about him. Not when they could look at Jessie.

Ki left the hotel long after dark, using the rear door to the stables. He rode away from the town on the hired horse, circled around to the road and went south, halting within sight of the lights in the Rollins house. He tied the animal off the road and crept close.

Only two rooms in the house were lighted; one was the kitchen, where the woman was mixing something in a pot. As Ki watched, the man, Rudd, came into the kitchen and sat at the table.

Ki watched them for an hour, till they finally went to bed and put all the lights out. Dutch was not there, nor were the others.

He moved to the barn. Inside he struck a match and looked in the four stalls. No horses. There were no horses in the outside corral either, only the two mules that had always been there. But, if Dutch and the gang had come from their boat, they would not have horses.

He went back to the front of the house and waited another hour. It was chilly and a light breeze came off the river, icy fingers poking into his clothes. He swore under his breath, mounted the horse and rode back to the hotel.

Jessie had long since gone to sleep. In the morning they conversed. Ki said, "They're probably off somewhere on the damned boat."

"Probably . . ."

"I think we're wasting our time here."

The holdup and murders on the steamboat *Cleo* aroused people up and down the river. Five killings were too much, the newspapers shouted in black headlines. Others said the governors of the several states ought to call out the militia. Exactly what the soldiers would do, they did not say. But calling them out was doing *something*. The law did not seem to be moving very fast. People were frustrated. The frustration led to foolish mistakes.

The law felt the pressure, and in order to appear to be moving ahead, politicians invited hordes of amateur volunteers to organize themselves into posses, armed with pictures of Dutch and descriptions of the others, Trask and Boles.

In the town of Warwick, a man was hauled off a horse. He resembled the picture of Dutch, and when he could not answer questions quickly enough because he stuttered in fright, a gang of men rushed him to the edge of town and hanged him from a tree limb.

It was discovered subsequently that he was a well-known farmer from the next county who had come to Warwick to buy mules.

Newspapers printed the shocking story and it dampened the hunt for Dutch. Men everywhere shaved their beards.

Karl Loder had taken his wife and family away from Grogan, in fear of Dutch's reprisal. They went to live with his wife's family in the next state. Then a friend wrote Karl that Dutch had burned down his house. Karl was enraged; he returned to Grogan alone.

He had built the house with his own hands, when he and his wife had married. It held so many memories . . . And now where the house had stood was only a blackened bit of ground. He almost cried, looking at it.

That Dutch had done it he did not doubt for a moment. No one else hated him enough to do such a thing. But Dutch forgot—two could play at that game.

Karl bought a tin of coal oil, and that night, long after midnight, he walked across the fields to the Rollins house. There was no moon; it was dark as the inside of a raccoon. The house too was dark, not a sound from within.

Dutch was not there, his friends had assured him, but old Rudd and Mae were. He had no quarrel with them, but unfortunately for them, they were caught in the middle.

He crept close to the house and splashed the coal oil over one entire side, from front to back. Then he drew his pistol and fired three warning shots through the front windows. At the same time, he struck a match and tossed it into the dripping oil. The fire skittered along the side of the house and flamed up, engulfing it in moments.

Karl emptied the pistol into the windows and in a few minutes saw Rudd and Mae scamper out the back and run to the barn. Rudd grabbed a pail, filled it with water from a horse trough and ran back to fling it on the roaring flames.

In the trees, well away from the house, Karl laughed at the puny effort. No one would get that conflagration out. The sparks were shooting high in the air, a beautiful sight. There was a lesson for Dutch . . .

Karl watched till the flames began to die. Several neighbors on horses galloped to the scene but could do nothing to help.

The house burned to the ground and lay smouldering. A fickle wind blew the smoke to Karl. He sniffed and walked back to his own house, hooked up his buckboard and departed.

An eye for an eye; a house for a house.

The news that Dutch's house had burned to the ground the night before was all over town in the morning, when Jessie and Ki went across the street to the restaurant for breakfast.

And since Karl Loder's house had burned down mysteriously—most believed by Dutch's hand—it took little imagination to consider that Karl had burned down Dutch's house. It was known that Karl had been in the town, though none could locate him that morning.

Rudd and Mae Rollins were reduced to living in the barn, which had not burned.

Karl Loder had had the last word. And no one in Grogan knew—or would admit he knew—where Karl had gone.

Jessie and Ki, in company with a few others, rode out to view the blackened remains. Rudd described to the gawkers that the arsonist had fired shots through the windows to awaken him and Mae. Otherwise they would have been roasted in their bed.

He had not had a glimpse of the firebug. However, Rudd said, he had found a tin that had contained coal oil, which the arsonist had used to start the blaze.

The local deputy listened to Rudd's story and his accusation, but there was no proof that Karl Loder had been near the house. He had tried to find Loder that morning, but the man was not in town. Nothing could be proved.

126

"Sure, I know he done it," he told Rudd. "But I can't prove it to a judge, can you?"

With Alley Trask at the wheel, they chugged downstream with no destination in mind. Alley was all for returning to New Orleans. They had a sackful of loot and jewelry to sell to old Isaac, and there was every sort of fun to be had . . .

Emory agreed with him, but Dutch was worried. There were too damned many posters everywhere with his picture on them. And every newspaper they read talked about the search and preached of the fire and brimstone the robbers would face in Hell. Some even said fire and eternal burning were too good for them.

"We ought to hole up somewheres for a month," Dutch said grumpily. "By then maybe they'll forget about us."

"Jesus! A month!" Emory said. "That's damn near for-ever!"

"Hangin's forever too," Dutch reminded him. "Another thing, we ought to paint a different name on this here boat. What you say?"

"Good idee," Alley agreed quickly. "We got plenty of paint."

"Then let's find us a place to tie up."

Emory asked, "What name shall we paint on?"

"I knew a gal named Caroline," Alley said. "That's a good name."

"It's too long," Emory objected. "How about Iris?"

Dutch smiled. "That's a nice short, easy name to paint."

Iris it was. They found a cove in a bend of the river and pushed in where trees hid them from midstream and the water was only waist deep. Emory was acknowledged the best hand, so he was delegated to do the painting. First he painted the name areas on both sides of the boat and let them dry overnight. The next day he painted "Iris" on both sides, where "Cynthy" had been.

And later they continued downstream.

It was late in the afternoon of the next day when they saw the steamboat in the distance. It was a smallish stern-wheeler, and it was in the center of the river and not moving.

127

Alley squinted at it. "I think it's aground on a sandbar." He grinned at Dutch. "Don't that look like a sittin' duck?"

Dutch grinned back. "It sure as hell does. Pull in alongside of her, like we're gonna help. But don't nobody show no guns till we're close in and look her over. If she got rifle guards on board, we just go on by."

"Yeah, right," Alley said, slowing the *Iris*.

As they came near they saw that the other boat, the *Hannah*, was heavily loaded and apparently had few passengers. The crew was in the act of getting out and placing the spars to grasshopper the boat over the sandbar.

As the *Iris* drifted close, faces turned toward them and a few people waved. They could see no men with rifles, and Dutch said softly, "Get in close and tie up to her, and we'll jump aboard."

"Right-o." Alley eased the *Iris* in, and Emory went forward and picked up a line. He tossed it to one of the men on the other boat. He tied it off and someone else tied the stern line.

Then, with drawn pistols, they jumped aboard the *Hannah*. Smiling faces turned to scowls at sight of them, and several men yelled. Dutch fired into the air, stifling the howls; then he lined them up and motioned to Alley.

Showing his teeth, Alley shook out a grain sack and went along the line, collecting valuables. "Empty your pockets, mister. I'll take that ring. You, lady, off with them earrings."

With Dutch and Emory menacing them, no one attempted to resist. Dutch could hear murmurs; they had recognized him.

When Alley was satisfied the passengers had given him all they had, he backed away and jumped to the *Iris*. Emory tossed off the lines, and with Dutch still holding two pistols on the *Hannah*, the *Iris* sheered away and headed downstream.

As Dutch ducked into the near cabin, several men from the upper deck of the *Hannah* fired at them. Bullets rapped into the hull and Dutch laughed. It had been the easiest haul they'd made yet.

But when they had left the other boat behind, Alley scowled. "All of them seen us—and the boat. They'll be lookin' for this steamer now, just when we changed the goddamn name."

"Well, we'll change it again."

Emory said, "Maybe we ought to get rid of the boat."

Dutch shook his head. "This's a hell of a long river, couple thousand miles anyway."

Alley agreed. "They must be hunnerds of boats like this one. We see 'em ever' day."

Dutch continued, "We can go up the Missouri for a spell. They don't know us there. You ever been to Omaha?"

"Or we can go down to New Orleans," Alley said. "That's a good five hunnerd miles from here. And we got lots of stuff for old Isaac."

"I vote for the Missouri," Dutch said.

He was quickly outvoted. "But before we go anywheres," Alley said, "let's change the name again."

They found a deep, wide stream flowing into the Mississippi, pushed the boat into it, around a bend, and tied it up. It took two days to paint on the new name. They settled on Cora, the name of a whore in Natchez that Dutch had been fond of.

It took three days to reach the levee at New Orleans. When they nudged in, Dutch and Emory took the loot in a carpetbag and went off to see Isaac. Alley stayed on board to watch things.

Johnson Baily received a cable from Elliot Scully. He would return to the states in about a month, Elliot said, if all things went well. Reading the wire, Baily blew out his breath. Things were not going well *here*. He had very little time.

And very few ideas.

Where did you find the kind of man who would play havoc with a steamboat line—and yet not run amok?

Maybe he could take things slowly, one at a time. Maybe such a man could be induced to do one job—then another, and another. Baily sighed. That was the way he'd worked with Dutch. Was there any other way? He had no idea of the criminal mind, as proved by his experience with Dutch. What the hell was his first move?

He took the bit in his teeth, stopped in a saloon on his way home and, on a sudden urge, asked one of the bartenders if

129

he knew a man who could act as a bodyguard.

"I want someone who is not afraid of anything and who is tough . . ."

The bartender wrinkled his brows. "Lemme talk to George in the back."

He returned in five minutes with a bit of paper and handed it over. "Here's a name. Ask for him at the Golden Horn."

The name was Axel Coyle. The Horn was a large saloon several miles south. Baily drove there and went inside, telling Henry to wait. He asked the first bartender he saw if he knew Axel Coyle. The man nodded and pointed him out, a big man sitting at a far table with a beer in front of him.

Baily went across the room. "Mr. Coyle . . ."

The big man looked him over. "Yes?" He had a curiously soft voice.

Baily sat down opposite him. "Perhaps we can have a little talk."

"What about?"

"Employment."

Coyle cocked his head. "You want to hire me?"

"Maybe. Shall we talk about it?"

Coyle sipped the beer. "Yeah. All right."

Baily glanced around the half-crowded room. "Can we go somewhere else?"

"Sure . . ." Coyle finished the beer and got up. He followed Baily out to the street.

Baily said, "We can talk in the carriage." He opened the door and Coyle got in. To Henry he said, "Just drive around a bit." He got in beside Coyle.

As he settled himself, Baily felt the pressure. He looked down and there was a gun in his side. He gaped at it and Coyle said, "Your money case—hand it over."

"But . . . we came to . . ."

"You ain't hirin' me, mister. Gimme the money or you're a dead man."

Baily did as he was told and sank back, his face ashen. God! What next!

Coyle rapped on the box and yelled at Henry to stop the coach. When it stopped he got out without a word to Baily.

130

Henry climbed down and looked in the door. "You all right, Mr. Baily?"

"Is he gone?"

Henry scanned the street. "Don't see 'im."

Baily sighed deeply. "Let's go on home."

★

Chapter 21

The holdup on board the steamboat *Hannah* was a big break in the case. Jessica and Ki read about it on the boat heading back to St. Louis.

Sergeant Tyler of the St. Louis police thought so too. He said, "All three of them were on the boat *Iris*. Dutch was recognized by everybody who saw him apparently. When the three of them left the *Hannah* they headed south. There'll be a hundred men waiting for them."

"*If* they continue south," Jessie said.

Tyler shrugged. "Yes, of course. If a lot of things happen, like if they get organized quickly."

Jessie said, "It's a break in the case in that now we know what kind of a boat they have, and her name." She looked at them quizzically. "Of course they'll change that."

"I suppose so."

Ki remarked, "They might even get rid of the boat . . . get another."

Tyler said, "You can't second-guess criminals. People like Dutch often do odd things. Besides, in order to organize a hunt, the police have to depend on the telegraph and most small towns aren't on the lines. It's a huge problem getting men to the right place at the right time. The area is too big. There are plenty of times you can't see across the river. They could be going upstream and the hunters going down, and never see each other."

Ki glanced at Jessie. "So maybe it's not all that big a break."

"Well," Tyler said, "we know more each time they rob a boat. Remember, not long ago we were wondering where Dutch was. Now we know."

Alley Trask bought several newspapers from a boy who was hawking them along the levee. One was a New Orleans daily, another was from Natchez. Both had similar stories concerning the robbery on board the *Hannah*.

And both had excellent descriptions of the steamboat *Iris*.

It was enough to make him very uncomfortable. Especially later when he noticed a blue-clad policeman eyeing the boat. The copper had a paper in his hand that he referred to, looking from it to the *Cora*.

Alley watched the man from the shelter of the pilothouse. The bluecoat moved closer and squinted at the name, and Alley bit his lips, wondering if the new paint was obvious. If the man got the idea that the name had been painted over . . .

He frowned as the policeman had a good long look at the boat, then turned on his heel and walked away. He disappeared in the press of wagons and the crowds of men and goods piled on the levee.

Alley did not hesitate. None of them had much of anything on board. He quickly filled a carpetbag with what he could find and jumped ashore. The copper would be back with others.

He hurried to Isaac Kupper's place of business. Dutch and Emory were still there, going over the various pieces with the old man.

He told them what he had seen, and Dutch swore. Emory said, "I'll go back and see what happens. You stay here. Is there anything on board with our names on it?"

"Nothing," Alley replied. "But they going to grab the boat."

"If they don't," Dutch said, "they'll watch it and grab us when we show up."

Emory left and wandered down the levee, looking like a hundred others. He leaned against a wagon and stared at the *Cora*. Half a dozen police were aboard, snooping about. Finally they left two men hidden aboard. The others scattered along the levee, mingling with the crowds. They would close in when the boat owners appeared.

Emory returned to Isaac's shop. They had lost the boat, he told them. The coppers were swarming about it, waiting for them to come back. "We best get out of town."

Isaac had a suggestion. He knew a man who hauled goods up and down the river on his small steamer. Isaac hinted that the man was in the smuggling trade and not averse to turning a shady dollar.

"He might take you upriver. He don't take passengers as a rule, but if I give you a note . . ."

"What's his name?"

"Augie, August Dorman. We knowed each other a long time."

"Thanks, Isaac."

"His boat's called the *Scout*, last time I knew. You watch the levee till he shows up."

The boat was not in New Orleans when they traversed the levee. They put up at two different boardinghouses under other names, and three days passed before the *Scout* appeared.

The newspapers were full of speculation about them, running the picture of Dutch with and without a beard and descriptions of the others. Dutch spent much of the time in his room, sleeping. He slipped out at night but stayed away from crowds and his usual haunts in the river city.

August Dorman and two black men ran the boat. Augie was a bulky, powerful man with white hair. He studied the note from Isaac and motioned them aboard.

"I take you. We go upriver tomorrow, soon's I get a load."

Dutch asked, "How far you go?"

"Past Baton Rouge a little bit. I put you off where you can get horses . . . or another boat. The police want you?"

134

Dutch nodded. Augie said, "Then you stay outa sight." He pointed to the cabin.

By the next afternoon, the *Scout* was loaded with farm tools in crates. Augie Dorman signed the papers, and the boat backed out into the stream and headed upriver.

Augie did not stop for nightfall; he merely reduced speed and plowed ahead confidently. He had made this run, he told them, hundreds of times and knew personally every drop of water and grain of sand.

He unloaded his cargo at two different plantation landings and, above Baton Rouge, told them the next stop was his last. He would put off the remaining cargo and turn back.

But before his final stop, he pulled at dusk to the bank where there were pilings and a landing of sorts. The town was inland, he said, a half dozen miles. He shook hands all round, and Dutch, Alley and Emory jumped off and watched the *Scout* disappear in the mists.

It was a long walk into town, a sleepy little burg, all locked up for the night. In the morning, they purchased three horses from a horse dealer, leaving town before most of the stores were open.

The road to the north left the river and wended its way through heavily forested land, often five or six miles, at their best estimate, from the river. Now and then, as the river made a huge bend, the road came to the very edge of the water. And occasionally they halted to watch a steamboat brush the trees, so close it came to the bank, following the changing channel.

For the first two days they met no one on the road. Then they came to a tiny settlement by the river, where there was a store and a deadfall along with a busy wood yard.

On the outside wall of the saloon was one of the posters—"REWARD!"—bearing Dutch's picture with the beard. He was clean-shaven now and pulled down his hat as he entered.

The only bartender was an older man with steel-rimmed glasses and very little hair. He served them beer and whiskey and went back to the end of the bar, where he sat with a newspaper.

But each time Dutch looked up, the man was staring at him. At Dutch's glance, he'd go back to the paper.

Dutch whispered to Alley, who got up and went down to the barkeep, asking if there was a lawman in town; he wanted to report a stolen animal.

The bartender replied that the nearest law was at Kaystown across the river. Another lawman on this side was at Kendall, about fifty miles east. Alley thanked him politely.

When they had finished the drinks, they went to the store to buy supplies. The storekeeper was middle-aged with a round belly and little blinking eyes. He toted up what they had bought and piled it into gunnysacks.

As they paid him, Emory asked about a road heading east. They were looking to go to Hattiesburg, he said.

"They's a road goes east through Kendall, maybe five-six mile north of here," the storekeeper told them. "They's traffic from the river goes that way."

They thanked him and departed without haste. But a mile along the road Dutch halted. "I think we maybe got trouble."

"The saloon man?"

Dutch nodded. "He knew me all right. That reward would make him a happy man."

Alley glanced around at the surrounding forest. "What you want to do, Dutch?"

Emory said, "You figger they going to ambush us?"

"They might. How long would it take one o'these country boys to make a thousand dollars?"

"Forever," Alley said. "They'll have to circle around to get ahead of us . . ."

"That's right." Dutch pointed. "Let's us head for the river, just cut right direct from here. That might throw 'em off."

Alley nodded. "Yeah, let's do it."

With Alley in the lead and each of them carrying a revolver in his hand, they walked the horses single file though the trees. They moved slowly, to make as little noise as possible, and saw no one. They halted now and then to listen, and they had to make a dozen detours to get around fallen trees or to cross deep ravines.

136

They did not come into sight of the broad river for more than an hour.

Alley grinned. "I think we give 'em the slip all right. If they was anyone after us . . ."

The sky was overcast and it smelled like rain. They looked for a path along the river and found none, but Alley suggested they follow the river the rest of the day. It was only a few hours till dark.

"We can cut back to the road in the morning."

The others agreed.

It was very slow going. They continued single file till dusk, then halted in a glade to make camp. Emory dug a deep hole for a tiny fire, which they put out as soon as they had heated meat and made coffee. Then they rolled in their blankets as the river mists stole through the trees toward them.

At first light they woke. Dutch was feeling edgy and wanted to go on at once. The woods hemmed them in, he said nervously, making him feel as if they were watched.

Alley calmed him somewhat, saying that no one could find them here; there was too much forest for anyone to hunt them down easily. He made another tiny fire in the same hole, and they ate breakfast and prepared to go.

Emory had used all his canteen water on coffee. "I'll go down and get some more."

He headed for the riverbank and had taken no more than two dozen steps before the shots came.

Dutch was watching Emory go and saw him flung down like a rag doll. He sprawled on the ground and never moved. Dutch yelled, reached for his pistol and ran for the horses. He and Alley fired shots into the woods where they thought the sniper had fired from.

They dug in their heels and galloped through the trees, ducking branches. A dozen shots came after them, slashing through the tree limbs but doing no harm.

In a mile or so, Dutch reined in and reloaded the Colt.

Alley said, "They fired too soon. When Emory showed himself, they shot at him before they was ready . . . or they'd a got all of us—maybe." He looked back. "You think Emory was dead?"

"I saw 'im hit. He was dead all right." Dutch sighed.

Alley shook his head, blowing out his breath. "Shit . . ."

They went on, bending back toward the road, and reached it an hour later.

Alley got down and examined the earth for a dozen feet. "It don't look like nobody's been here."

"They still behind us then," Dutch said, gazing back. "Let's keep moving."

They had left behind their blankets and he swore under his breath. Damn. No place was safe for him as long as those damned posters were everywhere.

The deadfall owner was Calvin Hanks. When he saw the three men come into his saloon and got a good look at one of them, he was positive it was Dutch Rollins. The latest news they had was that Dutch was somewhere in the vicinity—and here he was.

Hanks had studied one of the early posters, without the beard. It was Dutch all right. And the two with him matched the descriptions of Trask and Boles. Jesus! A lot of reward money was sitting there.

Hanks waited till they left, then called his son, Jamie, and told him who he had seen. "They was in the store and now they taking the road north. You'n Will get a-moving and get ahead of them. They's a thousand dollars on the line."

Jamie ran for his horse. He and Will were of a size, both dark and lean. They galloped into the woods, making a wide circle to avoid the road—they knew every inch of the land and knew an excellent place from which to ambush the strangers.

When they got to the place, the three had not yet arrived. Jamie and Will levered their Winchesters and talked about what they would do with their share of the reward.

Two hours passed and the three had still not shown up.

Something was wrong. Had his father made a mistake?

They got on their horses, went back along the road and, as the light began to fail, found the spot the three men had turned off to go toward the river.

They discussed it. They dared not go much farther—they might run into the pilgrims in the dark. The best thing was

138

to make a cold camp and wait till dawn. Their quarry would probably do the same thing.

At sunup they left the horses behind and ran silently through the woods with their rifles ready, expecting to find the strangers in a camp. As they approached the river they halted, listening. Jamie whispered, "I hear horses . . ."

It was brushy land, and they went on till they heard voices. Then one of the strangers suddenly appeared, walking toward the river with a canteen. Will raised his rifle and fired. The man dropped the canteen and crumpled . . .

Jamie swore at Will, but the damage was done. The other two dashed to their horses and galloped off, firing back at Jamie and Will.

It took forever to go back for their horses and then pick up the trail again. Jamie grumped at Will the entire time; it was his fault they had lost the rewards. Will said they still had the reward on one of them . . .

But they both knew the quarry was alerted and they probably would not get a second chance.

And worse, it began to rain.

★

Chapter 22

It was drizzling when they approached the crossroads the store owner had told them about. And it was farther than the five or six miles he had mentioned.

They had a choice of three directions.

Alley squinted at the sky. "Let's go to the river. We might be able to get a boat."

Dutch nodded, glancing behind them. As they turned west, it began to rain harder.

It was an hour's ride to the river, over an increasingly muddy road. On the bank were two shacks and a corral. An older man came to a doorway, a corncob pipe in his mouth.

"You lookin' to git acrost?"

"They told us there was a ferryboat here."

The old man pointed. "It comin' back in a while."

He told them that steamboats stopped here mostly to deliver goods, which he put in the other shack till the owners came for them. He was a sort of watchman.

They got down and waited in the old man's shack. After an hour or so the rain slackened and the ferryboat came chugging out of the mists, puffing steam from a tall pipe. It was a long, flat raft-like craft with railings on each side, two small paddle wheels and a steam engine to drive them, a very odd looking contraption.

A man and his son worked the power raft. They led the horses on board and tethered them fore and aft, then collected a dollar for each man and animal. After a long wait, during which time the young man stacked wood aboard, they pushed off again and headed for the far side.

The trip across was slow. The man angled the craft, and they reached the opposite shore some distance above the old man's shack.

There was a well-rutted road there, and they mounted and headed north again as it began to get dark.

Jamie and Will went back for the body of the man Will had shot and wedged it on Will's horse behind the cantle. They walked the horses to the settlement.

Jamie said, "In order to collect the reward, we got to haul the body to the law."

"Jesus! That'll take two days anyway."

"He going to stiffen up too. We'll put 'im on a mule."

Will said, "How much we get for this'n you figger?"

"I dunno . . ."

As Will had said, it took two days to reach Kendall with the body lashed to a mule, stiff with rigor. They went to the local deputy's office, and he directed them to the undertaker's, where he showed up with papers containing the descriptions of Dutch and his gang.

The body had a knife strapped on, and the haft had the initials EB carved on it. The deputy compared the face with the papers and decided it was probably the body of Emory Boles.

Jamie said, "My ol' man recognized Dutch Rollins. This here is one of his gang."

The deputy agreed to put through a voucher; it would take a while for payment. "You should've shot Dutch. He worth a hell of a lot more."

Jamie glared at Will. "Yeah . . ."

The newspapers, when they got hold of the story, made much of the shooting. Another of the Rollins gang had bit the dust.

141

In St. Louis a reporter speculated about the gang. Would Dutch quit now that he had only one man left? Or would he find others to take the place of the downed men? He should have no trouble picking up recruits . . .

When Jessie and Ki talked to him, Sergeant Tyler said, "I wish the damn newspapers would not keep telling Dutch how to run his affairs. They ought to shut up and let Dutch make mistakes. Be better for us."

Jessie mused, "I wish we could somehow set a trap for him . . ."

"Set a trap?"

"Well," she said, "remember Mr. Baily told us he used to send cash up the river in his steamboat's safes. If we spread the rumor there was cash in a boat's safe, would Dutch bite?"

Tyler smiled and shook his head. "Not practical . . . if only one boat was involved. And if a lot of boats suddenly were rumored to have cash in safes, even the dumbest robber would be suspicious, don't you think?"

She sighed. "I suppose so . . ."

Ki said, "Since you mention Baily, the newspapers also have printed items about his company. His stockholders are unhappy about the way the company is run."

"That's their business. We can't do nothing about that."

Ki shrugged. "I'm still wondering why Dutch tried to shoot him."

Tyler made a face. "Well, we asked him about that and Baily says he has no idea—if it was Dutch."

When Jessie and Ki went back to the hotel for supper, Ki said again, "It *is* damn curious that Dutch tried to kill Baily. There must be some connection between them."

"Sergeant Tyler doesn't think so."

"Yes, but Tyler must have two dozen other cases to worry about. Maybe more."

She smiled at him. "So what are you suggesting?"

"I'm thinking we ought to look into Baily's background. Who knows what we'll find?"

"Into his background?"

"Well, we know about Dutch's. And it hasn't helped."

She pursed her lips. "Where do you want to start?"

142

"Right here. You go into the Baily-Keller offices tomorrow and say you're thinking of investing in the company. Ask for more information about the company officers. It's a perfectly logical question."

"All right." She smiled. "I'll give it a try . . ."

She dressed demurely in black, with a short cape lined with dark green, and took a hack to the offices. Ki waited outside, and Jessie went in and talked to a clerk who ushered her into a small office. She was seated opposite a bright-looking young man who gazed at her appreciatively and asked how he could help her.

"I'm thinking of investing in the company. But I'd like to know more about it and the officers."

"Certainly, miss. We have several brochures . . ." He produced them with a flourish and handed them across the desk.

Jessica looked them over casually. "I see Mr. Baily is president . . . but there's not much of a biography here."

"I'm sorry." The clerk tried his most winning smile. "That was given to us by Mr. Baily. No one has questioned it before . . ."

She thanked him, took the papers and departed to meet Ki on the street. He read the biography. "It says he was born in Baltimore, Maryland, and attended Haycroft College." He glanced at her. "Let's start there."

"You want to go there?"

"Let's start with a telegram. We can ask for details about him. That should be a routine request."

They sent the telegram and in three hours received a reply. Johnson Baily was unknown at the college. No one by that name had ever been registered.

Jessie said, "He may have used a different name."

"Maybe Johnson is a middle name . . ."

"Yes. Let's suggest that."

They tried the college again, but the reply came back very definitely. No one with the name Baily had ever attended the institution.

"Very interesting," Ki said. "Do you suppose he's lying?"

Jessie looked at him. "Do you suppose Johnson Baily is not his real name?"

"That's possible. I suggest we should hire a man to go there and see what he can unearth."

"I agree . . ."

They hired Eric Allen, a man who advertised himself as an investigator. He was small and dapper, clean-shaven, with eyes like a wren's quick and dancing. He frowned over the brochures and agreed to leave for Baltimore at once. He would wire them daily . . .

Three days later they came to Grogan from the south and got down in front of the Rollins barn. Dutch was astonished to see the house had burned to the ground!

Rudd said, "That sombitch Karl Loder done it."

"Is he here in town?"

Rudd shook his head. "Nobody knows where he gone to."

Mae said, "He took the family and all."

They had fixed up a room at the back of the barn as living quarters. It had a plank floor, four walls and a door and was kitchen, parlor and bedroom, all in one.

They sat at a rickety table while Mae boiled coffee. Rudd wanted to know where Emory had got to, and they told him what had happened. They had managed to skin out, but Emory had been unlucky.

"Too bad," Rudd said sadly. "What you going to do now, Dutch?"

"Find us another man'r two."

"What happened to your boat?"

"Goddamn police in New Orleans got it. We had to skin out of there too. Them damn posters makin' life miserable. Me and Alley, we figger to hole up here for a spell. Let things cool off."

Alley asked, "You going to build the house again?"

Rudd sighed. "Hell, take two hunnerd dollars to build a house. I dunno . . ."

"Build it," Dutch said. He counted out the money as Mae and Rudd smiled.

★

Chapter 23

When next Rudd went to the general store in town, he took the buckboard. He had a long list, much longer than usual, and carried four heavy sacks of food out to the wagon.

Roy Green watched him from the shelter of a bench by the Two Barrels. When Rudd climbed to the seat, turned the wagon around and walked the mule out of town, Roy got up and wandered into the store.

He talked to the owner, Kissler, passing the time of day, then said, "That Rudd, he sure eats good for a skinny one, don't he?"

"Yeah, he does. But nobody holds a candle to ol' Miz Birwell. I bet you that woman eats five times a day. Look at her—you believe it?"

"Yeah, I do. But she ain't skinny like Rudd." He noticed the list on the counter and edged closer.

Kissler went to move some kegs, and Roy picked up the list, studying it. There was enough vittles there for a squad of men. He fingered his unshaven shin. Maybe Dutch was out there . . .

He left the store and wandered back to his bench. How much was the reward on Dutch anyways? And there was a reward on

145

the others, Emory and Alley Trask. A hell of a lot of money. Enough money for a man to get the hell out of Grogan and go somewhere back east. Roy stared at the road Rudd had taken. He would never in his life see that much money unless . . . Roy smiled and sighed. Unless . . .

That night, long after dark, he walked down the road to the Rollins barn. It was no trick at all to see that Dutch *was* there. Roy crept close enough to smell the beans Dutch was eating.

The next day, Roy borrowed a boat, saying he wanted to do a little fishing. He rowed across the river, sent a telegram and rowed back, forgetting to fish. He spent the rest of the day counting the money he was going to get when they hauled Dutch in.

Eric Allen made his first report four days later. He had arrived in Baltimore and had a long session with the city registrar.

There were eight families with the name Baily—none, however, with the first name Johnson.

"Very peculiar," Ki said, reading the wire. "Apparently the man has no roots."

"If Baily isn't his real name, why would he change it?"

"To hide something?"

Jessie shrugged.

They talked to Sergeant Tyler the next day. He had received word from an informant that Dutch was in Grogan again. They met Tyler in the little park, and he told them his department had pulled Hank Summers away and sent him on other duty.

"So we can't confirm the report that Dutch is there. Summers is no longer in Grogan. We know that Dutch and the others lost their steamboat in New Orleans . . ."

Jessie asked, "Are you going to act on the information?"

Tyler made a wry face. "My superiors say no. But we've sent the particulars along to people closer to Grogan. Let them handle it. My bosses say they went along once, but not again. It costs money to send men that far downriver and back."

They received another wire from Eric Allen in Baltimore. He had decided to try variations of the name Baily and had turned up a John Bailor. He was in the process of tracking the man down.

Jessica and Ki took the next steamboat south and got off at Grogan. However, they were too late. The operation to capture Dutch had been run—and Dutch had not been found.

It was the main subject of conversation in the town. The police had been under the command of a sheriff from across the river; his name was Horace Evans, and he was generally considered to be a first-class bungler. He had definitely bungled the job in Grogan. He had failed to surround the Rollins property and thus had allowed Dutch to ride away, thumbing his nose at the law.

Evans, they said, was a laughing stock even to his own men. The tipplers in Grogan said that if his opposition ran a mule against him in the next election, the mule would win.

To Jessie and Ki it was a disappointing trip. No one had the slightest idea where Dutch had got to.

They rode out to the Rollins property and found Rudd and another man leveling the ground with a mule team and a heavy log. He was going to rebuild the house, Rudd told them. And no, he had no idea where Dutch might be. "Maybe he gone down to New Orleans."

"He never gave you any indication?"

"Well maybe," Rudd said, with the innocent look of a river gambler, "he went over to Kansas City. He talked about that once."

Dutch learned about the second attempt to corral him almost as soon as it got started. Sam at the saloon sent a boy out to warn him that some men were coming across the river. He and Alley rode away from the barn into the woods, and when the lawmen got tired of questioning Rudd and Mae and left the way they'd come, he and Alley rode back.

But Dutch was very curious. "How'd they know I was here?"

Rudd said, "Somebody must've seen you."

"Who?"

"How the hell I know?"

Dutch persisted. "Did you talk to anybody when you went into town for vittles?"

"Only to Kissler in the store, but you wasn't mentioned. Hellsfire, Dutch! I ain't gonna tell nobody you's here!"

"I know you ain't. Did you see anybody in town lookin' at you crossways?"

"I didn't see nobody in town." Rudd frowned and paused. "Well, I seen old Roy Green asettin' by the saloon."

"Roy talk to you?"

"No."

"He didn't come into the store?"

"No. He didn't come in and he didn't foller me."

Alley asked, "Who's Roy Green?"

"A no-account," Rudd said. "Forget him."

But later, away from the barn, Dutch said, "That Roy, he's a back stabber."

"What could he do?"

"He could tell the law we's here." Dutch pulled his ear. "He'd have to go across the river to do it . . ." He went back to the barn and took Rudd aside. "You go find out if Roy got into a boat since you went into town."

"You think he sent a wire?"

"Yeah, I do."

Rudd hooked up a mule to the buckboard and rode into town again. When he came back hours later, he nodded to Dutch as he put the mule into the corral.

"He borrowed Perly Sim's boat, Dutch. Said he was goin' fishing."

Dutch smiled. "Did he bring back any fish?"

"Perly says he didn't."

They walked into town late that night, Dutch and Alley, and eased up to the door of the Two Barrels. Roy Green was sitting in his usual place in the corner, listening to the chatter. Dutch pointed him out.

"That's the little piece o' dog shit."

They waited till Sam closed the saloon. When Roy came out, they took his arms, one on each side, and walked him along the dark street.

Roy yelped, and Dutch said, "Shut up, or I swat you."

148

"Where you takin' me! What the hell this about, Dutch?"

"Shut up."

They walked him a mile out of town and turned him loose. Dutch drew his pistol.

Roy's eyes got big. "What the hell! What the hell you doin', Dutch?"

"I think you brought the law on me, Roy."

"I did no such thing!"

"I think you did."

"How'd I do that, for crissakes?"

"You borrowed Perly's boat and went across the river to the telegraph."

"All I did was go fishin'!"

"Issat all?"

" 'Course it is."

Dutch seemed to reconsider. He glanced at Alley, who shrugged. Dutch said, "All right, Roy. You go on home." He put the pistol back in his belt.

Roy took a deep breath and nodded. "Yeah, Dutch."

"Go on."

Roy turned and hurried toward town.

Dutch let him get ten or twelve paces away and shot him three times in the back.

A farmer heading into town found the body next morning and hauled it to the undertaker's parlor.

Ki heard the gossip in the hotel and went into the nearest saloon to hear more. Someone had shot Roy Green in the back last night and speculation was high that Dutch Rollins had done it—to shut Roy's mouth forever. Everyone knew that Roy was a shiftless little sneak. Perly said that Roy had borrowed his boat and had probably gone across the river to wire the law. Dutch had found out and had shot him.

No one had seen Dutch or knew where he was.

Ki said to Jessie, "Nobody doubts Dutch shot the man. They think it was Roy who wired the law . . . and it probably was."

"So Dutch is hiding out somewhere in the vicinity?"

"He may be. There's plenty of places. But we'll never find him, and I doubt if the law will mount another big search for him here."

"No, I suppose not."

If they were to remain in the steamboat robbing trade, Dutch said, they had to have at least one more man. Two would be better.

Four altogether would be best, Alley agreed. Four pairs of eyes to watch for trouble were a great deal better than two.

But where would they find two more men willing to share that kind of life?

"In New Orleans," Dutch said. "We can find anything we want there. Maybe old Isaac can help us. Remember he sent us to Augie Dorman."

Alley felt much the same way.

They stole a small boat several nights later, hoisted the sail, and Alley took the tiller as Dutch pushed off.

They stopped at Natchez, glad to get out of the boat and glad to see that some of the same girls were working the saloons . . .

But they pushed off for New Orleans when Dutch got edgy.

Issac was happy to see them when they appeared, but he might have been more joyful if they had brought items for sale. They explained that they'd lost Emory and had to replace him.

"It's a chancy business you're in," Isaac said, shaking his head. "Let me think on it . . . I know a few people . . ."

They took rooms in a boardinghouse and never stayed for meals. They avoided all contact with people, and on the third day, Isaac had a name for them.

"Virgil Finerty." He gave them an address. "He's just out of jail and expecting you."

"What you know about him?"

"He was in for theft. He's about nineteen and a little wild—"

"How do you know him?"

"Through a customer. Go look at him. Talk to him. If you don't like him . . . ," Isaac shrugged, "we find you somebody else."

150

"All right," Dutch said.

They found Virgil in a rundown section of town; he had a miserable little room in a smelly house. It had a cot bed, a scrap of rug on the floor, a washstand and some nails in the wall to hang clothes on.

Virgil was shorter than either of them, very pale and dressed almost in rags. When he let them in, he sat on the floor; they sat side by side on the sagging cot.

He grinned at Dutch, "I heard a lot about you."

"Yeah?" Dutch said, pleased.

"You're a big name on the river now."

Alley said, "Can you handle a gun, kid?"

"A pistol? Yeah."

"You own one?"

Virgil shook his head.

"You know what we do," Dutch said. "Does it scare you?"

Virgil looked surprised. "Hell no . . ."

"What were you in jail for?"

"I got a raw deal. We robbed a store and I got caught. My partner got away on a horse and didn't wait for me."

"You know 'im?"

"Yeah. I'll see him one of these days." He shook his closed fist.

Dutch got up and moved to the door. "All right, kid . . ."

"Hey, you goin' to take me along?"

"We got to talk." Dutch indicated Alley. "You go see Isaac tomorra afternoon." He opened the door.

In the street Dutch said, "So what you think?"

"I figger he'll do. We can try him out anyways. If he acts too smart, we get rid of him."

"Yeah, that's what I think," Dutch said.

"We were gonna hole up for a while. You still want to do that?"

"It's a good idee. But we're short of money. Now we got another hand, maybe we ought to fill our pockets."

"I like the sound o'that . . ."

★

Chapter 24

When they returned to St. Louis, two wires were waiting for them from Eric Allen. The first said he had visited all the local public offices and had located an address for John Bailor.

The second said he had gone to that address and talked to two people who lived in the house and who remembered Bailor. Bailor had been taken away by the police. As far as they knew, he had served five years in a federal prison. They did not know where he had gone after that.

Allen said he would visit the prison and hoped to get a photograph of Bailor.

The next morning the photograph arrived in the mail. It was a picture of the man they knew as Johnson Baily. He was then about twenty-five years of age. There was no doubt about it.

"He was in prison!" Jessica said. "Was he in jail with Dutch? Maybe something happened to make Dutch want to shoot him."

"No . . . Dutch is much younger. I doubt they would have been in prison together. When Baily was twenty-five, Dutch would have been nine or ten."

"Yes, I suppose so . . ."

Along with the photo was a note from Allen. It said that Baily/Bailor had gone to prison because of a merchandising scandal. He had been one of several accused of manipulating funds and causing a business firm to fail. He'd been convicted and had served most of a five-year sentence. It was after he'd gotten out that he'd changed his name.

Jessie wrote to Eric Allen at once, expressing their delight at his excellent work, and enclosing a bonus draft.

Ki said, "Do you think we ought to inform Sergeant Tyler of this? It will certainly change his opinion."

"It's just background; it's not evidence of anything."

"It shows a criminal bent, doesn't it?"

She shrugged lightly. "It doesn't answer the question of why Dutch shot at him."

"True . . ."

"And it doesn't show a connection of any kind between him and Dutch."

Ki said, "It makes us suspicious."

"Suspicious that Baily is still a crook?" She smiled. "Maybe he learned his lesson and is now a pillar of the church."

"And I'm Bonnie Prince Charlie."

Jessie laughed.

They took advantage of Augie Dorman's boat again. He carried them nearly a hundred miles above Baton Rouge this time. He had to deliver a half dozen unmarked crates. When Virgil asked what was in them, Augie merely smiled.

He nudged the *Scout* to the bank a mile south of a wood yard, at Dutch's request, and turned back.

When the boat had disappeared in the night, Dutch said to Virgil, "We go aboard the first boat that comes along without rifle guards on her. Me and Alley holds pistols on them, and you take the feed sack and get their goods. You unnerstand?"

"Why me with the sack?"

"Because I say so."

Virgil grumped, but he took the pistol Dutch handed him, looked it over and shoved it into his belt.

Alley had been prowling along the riverbank. He called to them, and when they joined him they saw the boats, three of

153

them tied to pilings. They smelled of fish.

Alley said, "This's how we get away."

There was a broad path leading from the river into the darkness. "Probably a house'r two back in there," Dutch said.

They went on through the trees to the wood yard. It was a larger establishment with three shacks, a corral and several blacks sitting around a fire amid stacks of cut wood. There was a murmur of voices from one of the shacks and a cackle of laughter.

Dutch said softly, "Sit down and wait."

Virgil sat but moved restlessly, and when a steamboat whistled and nudged into the pilings, he was eager to jump up. Dutch held him back. "It don't feel right . . ."

Virgil growled that it looked all right to him. Dutch and Alley exchanged looks. Was this kid going to be a pain in the ass?

The boat took on a load of wood and departed.

Hours later another steamer slid into the landing with much yelling. The roustabouts tied her off stem and stern, and the men started loading with rhythmic chanting.

Alley whispered, "No guards I c'n see . . ."

Dutch nodded. "Yeah, me neither. Let's go."

The mate shouted when he saw them, and Dutch fired two shots into the air to get everyone's attention. "Stand still, all you folks! You there, stan' still and shut up!"

Alley watched the upper deck, and Dutch motioned Virgil to reap the harvest with his sack. He held the cocked pistol on the muttering crowd.

Virgil went among the passengers, grabbing watches and prodding people with his gun muzzle when he thought them too slow.

A well-dressed older passenger seemed confused at Virgil's orders, and Virgil slapped at him with the pistol, knocking him back into the crowd, his face bloody. A woman screamed then, and someone fired a shot that smashed a lantern near Dutch.

Virgil fired back, his bullet rapping into a bulkhead. A boat's officer ran to the downed man, and Virgil whirled and shot him, eyes wild.

154

Men began to yell in anger, and Virgil backed away and fired deliberately into the crowd before Dutch grabbed him, shoving him toward the gangplank, shouting into his ear.

Virgil jerked away, thumbing the hammer on the pistol, firing again, and Alley suddenly came down with his gun barrel on the back of Virgil's head. He grabbed the sack, and he and Dutch ran into the night, leaving Virgil sprawled facedown, half on and half off the planks.

The steamboat *Montcalm* arrived in St. Louis, and the captain sent off a man to the police. They had one of Dutch Rollins's gang aboard, tied hand and foot!

Police arrived to surround the boat, and Sergeant Tyler hurried aboard. The man was well bound and had a nasty wound on the head; he was still unconscious. He had been hit by one of the gang, the captain told Tyler, and left behind.

"He's the one who killed three people," a passenger said. "He jus' went crazy!"

"And wounded two more," the captain added. "We've got a dozen witnesses."

Tyler was surprised. "The others left him behind?"

"That's right. This one went into a panic and started shooting, and they up and slugged him. I saw it all myself." The captain shook his head sadly. "One of the passengers was a little drunk and didn't understand what he was told and got hit. That started it."

"And you recognized Dutch?"

"We all did," someone said.

"Absolutely," the captain agreed. "Couldn't have been anyone else."

Tyler had the prisoner taken to a nearby hospital, then to jail, well bandaged. His name, according to effects in his pocket, was Virgil Finerty. He had a police record and had spent time in a New Orleans jail, for all his youth.

Virgil lay on a cot in his cell, conscious and grumpy.

Tyler came. "Why'd they leave you behind, Virge?"

"I dunno, the bastards!"

"Guess they didn't like you much. We got you to rights, kid. You're going to swing—instead of them."

Virgil glowered at him.

"Where'd they go?"

"I dunno."

"Hey, you going to hang all alone, Virge? You ought to have some company on that trip. Where'd they go?"

"They didn't tell me."

"Where'd you meet them?"

"In New Orleans."

"And they didn't say where they'd go after the robbery?"

"They had a boat ready. I guess they went downstream."

"They didn't mention a place?"

"No."

"How'd you get together with them anyway?"

"Through an old man, Isaac Kupper."

"Oh . . . Isaac, huh!" Tyler made a note. "I know who he is."

The newspaper made much of the capture. It was the first time that anyone of the notorious gang had been taken alive.

Tyler met Jessica and Ki in a restaurant. "He was a new recruit," Tyler said. "He replaced Emory Boles. This was his first job with them."

"And they got rid of him in a hurry," Ki said.

"Well, he's a mean little snot," Tyler said, shaking his head. "I don't blame them. Apparently he went into a panic on the boat and started shooting into the crowd. That's probably why they knocked him out. When shooting starts, it's anybody's chance to get killed. It's lucky that more people weren't hurt."

Jessie observed, "So they still need another man if they're going to continue . . ."

"Yes, I'd say so. Two men to rob a steamboat is cutting it too fine. Two men couldn't watch everyone."

Ki said, "Then they may not rob another boat for a while, till they find someone. And chances are they'll be more choosy."

Tyler grinned. "Exactly."

Jessie asked, "Did the prisoner tell you where they planned to go after the robbery?"

"No. He said he didn't know. But I suspect it'll be New Orleans. They had a boat waiting, Virgil said. He also mentioned Isaac Kupper, who's a suspected fence."

Jessie and Ki talked it over and decided to go to New Orleans themselves. She wired Denis Foucaud they were coming and bought passage on the steamer *Amelia*.

Dutch and Alley ran into the dark. There was no pursuit, but they could hear the excitement for a dozen minutes as they made their way through the trees. They found the boat, and jumped in and pushed off. Alley steered with an oar, and they glided away downstream, silent as a whisper.

When they were well away, Dutch growled. "The little son of a bitch! I never liked him much when we seen him . . ."

"Well, they goin' to hang him now, sure as hell."

"We didn't tell him nothing, did we?"

"About us?" Alley shook his head. "Nothing he can tell them except one thing."

"What's that?"

"The fact that Isaac sent him to us. So we'd better stay away from Isaac. The coppers will be watching his place."

Dutch frowned. "Maybe we can meet him somewhere."

It was a long, weary journey down the winding Mississippi in the small boat. But it attracted no attention; there were hundreds of boats on the river. They stopped at a number of river towns for food, tobacco and an occasional bottle. They also bought newspapers and read about Virgil Finerty. He blamed everything on Dutch Rollins, saying that Dutch had ordered him to fire into the crowd and he had done it reluctantly, fearing that Dutch or Alley would kill him if he did not.

Both Dutch and Alley were aghast and disgusted by the kid's story. What a liar he was! Dutch wanted to write to the newspapers with their side of the story, but Alley talked him out of it.

They gauged the trip so that they would arrive in New Orleans at night and slipped into town, leaving the boat on the levee. The next day, they sent a messenger with a letter to Isaac and received a reply saying the police had been around to question him. Isaac was sure the shop was under police surveillance. He advised them to stay away.

★

Chapter 25

Hap Stoker returned to St. Louis, very unhappy, and reported to Johnson Baily. He had no luck at all in tracing Dutch and was forced to give up the search. Clues were too few and far between, and the land was too vast. The mighty river provided thousands of hiding places; even with an army, he could never hope to dig Dutch out of his hole. By the time he reached the spot where Dutch had last been seen, the quarry was long gone and had usually left no trail. The thousand dollar bounty had dangled before his eyes long enough. Dutch was a will-o'-the-wisp.

To these arguments Baily had to nod, sighing inside. He'd had hopes for Stoker. He offered to up to the ante, but Stoker shook his head. He had to return to his own business, admitting that he was not a detective.

Baily saw him out. But he had his own troubles, large troubles. The people who worked for him saw an immense change; Baily had become nearly impossible of late. No one knew why.

Elliot Scully was the reason.

Scully would arrive in town very soon, expecting that their agreement had been fulfilled. Scully was not a man to fool with. He had come up the hard way, from field hand to deck hand on a steamboat to captain; he was hard as nails and quick to judge. He was rich and powerful and capable of almost anything. He would demand repayment of the money he had advanced to Baily—and Baily did not have it.

It meant that Scully would take over the Baily-Keller Line and he, Baily, would be out in the cold with nothing.

Nothing.

Of course he had prepared himself for Scully's arrival—or he thought he had. He had a hundred excuses and reasons why he had not carried out his part of the bargain.

But when the day came, when his clerk ran a boy upstairs to say Scully was in the building, he trembled and shook and had to get a grip on himself. He told himself over and over that he wasn't afraid of Scully . . .

But he was.

Elliot Scully was a big man in his late fifties but powerfully built, with hands twice as big as Baily's. He was also loud and overbearing. He liked to threaten people, to see them scurry. He came into Baily's office with a scowl.

"You haven't kept your agreement, Baily!"

"I . . . I . . . did m-my best to—"

"Your best stinks!" Scully advanced on him, face red. His huge fist slammed down on the desk and Baily jumped.

"You had months to do what we talked about. Months, for crissakes!" He pounded the desk again. An inkwell tipped over and black ink pooled on the papers there.

Baily squeaked, and Scully, his rage increasing, came around the desk.

Baily clawed a drawer open, grabbed a revolver and fired as fast as he could work the hammer. He saw Scully stagger back and fall, and he fired again, then dropped the pistol from nerveless fingers.

He fell into a chair, chest heaving, staring at the body on the floor as people crowded into the office, gaping at him.

Lieutenant Denis Foucaud came to the hotel and they had drinks in the bar. He had received routine information from St. Louis, he said, about a fence named Isaac Kupper. Kupper

159

was apparently the man who had brought Dutch together with Virgil Finerty.

"So we expect that Kupper knows something about Dutch."

"Yes, I'd think so," Jessie said.

"Kupper has a shop on Enright Street, and we've suspected for some time that he fences stolen goods. But it's not easy to prove. He's a very clever man."

Ki said, "You think he is buying the items Dutch and the others steal from steamboat passengers?"

"Certainly we do. But removed from its setting, one diamond or opal looks very much like another. He melts down the settings, so when we search the shop we find nothing incriminating."

"You've got men watching the shop?"

"Yes. We're hoping Dutch will walk in one day." Denis sighed deeply. "Really only a forlorn hope . . . But it has to be done."

Ki said, "So you think Dutch may be here in the city?"

"Yes, there's a good chance of it. Finerty said they had a boat ready to use after the last robbery. So, after the lead about Kupper, we think they're here." Denis shrugged. "Of course we haven't the manpower to investigate every hotel and rooming house in New Orleans . . ."

Jessie asked, "Does this man, Kupper, come and go, or does he live over the store?"

"He lives behind the shop, lives alone. He seldom goes out. A boy delivers a box of food to him each week . . . or more often."

Ki said, "Does he have a lot of customers?"

"A lot of people visit the shop, yes."

Jessie remarked, "If he lives behind the shop, then there are two doors?"

"Yes." He smiled at her. "We're watching both of them."

In his note to Isaac Kupper, Dutch had mentioned the items they had for sale, and Isaac sent a reply, asking for a meet. He suggested a certain house on Fenwick Street, not far from the shop. The house was owned by a relative and was unoccupied at the moment and also in an ideal location for their purpose, having half a dozen ways to enter and exit, much the same as Isaac's own shop and living quarters.

He would come late at night, Isaac said, and would evade the police in that manner.

The rear door of Isaac's quarters faced a maze of walls, vines and other doors, sheltered nooks and walks. It was a neighborhood of rooming houses and ancient buildings; many rooms had been built on after the houses had been lived in for decades, so that the area was a rabbit warren. One had to know his way around or become lost, especially at night, when there were no lights at all.

The several policemen who were assigned to watch Isaac's rear door were not at all certain they were in the right place. None of the doors had any identifying marks or numbers, and it was impossible for a stranger to know which door connected to the shop.

This was most of the reason Isaac had established his shop in that particular place. Many of his clients preferred dark and shady ways and traded with Isaac because of his location.

Isaac easily slipped away and met Dutch and Alley. He brought a glass and tools with him, and when Dutch dumped out the jewelry on a table, he sorted through it as before. In several hours, they agreed on a price, and he paid over the cash.

But the next morning Lieutenant Foucaud and a squad of men raided Isaac Kupper's shop. It happened that Isaac had not yet removed all the stones from their settings, or melted down the metal, so that there were names and inscriptions—evidence of robbery—etched and engraved in the silver and gold.

Isaac was taken into custody.

He implicated Dutch and Alley at once.

They had returned to their rooming house that same night and in the morning held a council of war. They sat by an outside window as far from the door as possible and talked in whispers. Now they had money. What was their next move?

Alley said, "We need somebody to take Virgil's place."

"Yeah, but who do we know?"

"Nobody we can trust. But we didn't know Virgil . . ."

"And look what happened," Dutch said bitterly. "Both of us coulda been killed."

"What if we leave the river?"

"Leave the river?" Dutch was astonished. "Where the hell would we go?"

"We could go back east."

"You know somebody there?"

"No . . ." Alley sighed deeply. "We got money, Dutch. We deserve some fun. I ain't had a girl in months."

"We dassent go back to the Cat."

"No, but there's other places. And there's Natchez."

Dutch nodded, thinking of the girls they'd seen the last trip there. A cute little brown-eyed minx came to mind. He grunted. "Maybe Augie Dorman is in town."

"Let's find out."

They had separate accommodations because each room had only one single cot. After Dutch had gone to his room, Alley sat on the bed and counted his money. He had almost nine hundred dollars in his kick, and it was burning a hole in his pants. As he fingered it he thought of the Silver Chord, a saloon near the waterfront, not a long way from where he sat. He could be there in twenty minutes, looking the girls over.

As he'd said, he hadn't had a girl in longer than he cared to think about. But it was not yet midnight. He could have one of those whore girls inside an hour if he wanted to. And Dutch didn't even have to know.

He hid most of the money in his room, opened the window as silently as he could and slid out to the grass and weeds. He closed the window and hurried around the house to the street.

In twenty-five minutes he was stepping inside the saloon. It was half-crowded, blue with smoke and lamp-oil smelly. He found a place at the long bar and ordered beer, sipping it as he looked around.

There were half a dozen painted girls in the room, some by the monte table and another coming toward him. She moved in and rubbed her thigh against him. "I ain't seen you in here b'fore, honey."

"I jus' got in town. What's your name?" She was round, with deep cleavage in front; her dress was black with ruffles and lace.

"Alisa," she said, moving her thigh suggestively. "What's yours?"

"Fred."

"You lookin' for fun, Freddie?"

"Yeah. How much you cost?"

"Well, it depends . . . let's go upstairs and talk about it, huh?"

"Yeah. Why not."

Two hours after midday, Lieutenant Foucaud had a visitor. A deck sergeant brought the girl in. She was pale and looked to be about thirty, Foucaud thought. She wore a satin dress under a long coat, and he wondered if she were in the whore trade. He gave her a chair in his office and closed the door.

"Yes, miss?"

"I come about the reward," she said.

"Oh? Which reward?"

"The one on Dutch Rollins."

Foucaud stared at her. "You know where Dutch is?"

"Well, no . . . but one of them others come to see me last night. He got a little drunk and mentioned about Dutch. Said him and Dutch was close."

"Where was this?"

"At the Silver Chord."

"Ahhh. You work out of there?"

She hesitated, and he said quickly, "I don't care if you do. What's your name?"

"Alisa Pascali."

"Tell me about this man."

She described Alley Trask. "He said his name was Fred. He had plenty of money to spend . . ."

"But you don't know where he lives?"

"No. You're the copper. You got to find him."

Foucaud smiled. "We will, Miss Pascali."

She rose. "This's secret, huh? He won't find out I told you and come and kill me?"

163

"Certainly not." He smiled reassuringly. "Everything you've told me is confidential. But please don't mention it to anyone yourself."

"I won't." She went to the door. "When do I get the money?"

"When he's arrested and convicted."

She sighed, nodded and went out.

Foucaud stationed a good man at the saloon immediately, in case "Fred" showed up again.

He saw Jessica and Ki for lunch and told them what the girl had said. "So it's very likely Dutch and Alley are in the vicinity. Alley probably picked that saloon because it was handy. I've got men out now canvassing the area."

Jessie said, "We'd like to be in on the capture, Denis . . ."

"I understand." He smiled. "Since I'm in charge, I can arrange it."

He was as good as his word. Two days later his men turned up two boarders who, a rooming house owner said, resembled the description of Alley and the picture of Dutch. Denis sent word to Jessie and Ki, giving them the address.

When they hurried there, a dozen policemen were in position, waiting Foucaud's order to close in on the house.

Denis said to Jessie, "We think they may still be in the house. The owner and others have come out quietly." He motioned, and the police advanced on the building, cutting off all retreat. Then a sergeant, at Foucaud's nod, shouted to Dutch and Alley to come out.

★

Chapter 26

There was no reply.

The sergeant repeated the order. Still no reply.

Ki said, "Are you sure they're in there?"

"No, not positive. The owner thought they were." Denis motioned and the uniformed policemen moved in closer. Several stepped up onto the porch.

Ki said to Jessie, "If they're not in the house, where would they be?"

"At the river." She turned to Denis. "We're going to the levee."

Denis nodded and followed his men to the porch. One opened the door and they slipped inside.

Jessie and Ki hurried to the river. Dutch would probably force his way onto a boat and head up or down stream as the quickest way out of the city. Would they be able to stop him?

They had to find him and Alley first. When they reached the levee, Jessie said, "Shall we separate?"

"No!" Ki said definitely. "We stay together." He looked along the line of busy steamboats that were loading and unloading. "If we're right, that he came here, he won't pick one of the big passenger boats—he's too well known."

She pointed. "There're some smaller boats. Three in a row."

Ki nodded and led the way toward them, threading between wagons and piles of crates and barrels. The smaller boats were the *Argus*, the *Scout* and the *Angelina*.

Ki halted near the first. It was taking on heavy wooden boxes; men stacked them on the afterdeck at the direction of a big, blue-coated man.

On the second boat, the *Scout*, there was no activity at all. It had steam up, and a man with a visored cap came from a cabin and stared off to his right. Jessie looked and saw he was gazing at one of the regular police who patrolled the levee. The man on board spoke to someone over his shoulder, and she saw a shadowy figure—did it resemble Dutch?

A crewman tossed off the lines, and the *Scout* began to back into the stream.

Jessie said to Ki, "Dutch is on that boat."

"Did you see him?"

"No—it's a hunch." The boat reversed the paddle wheel and began to move upstream.

Ki frowned at the *Angelina*. Two men were sitting on her foredeck in chairs, smoking pipes. She did not have steam up. Jessie's hunches were often good . . . He said, "We'd better get Denis."

They started back toward the house and met Denis and five men running to the levee. The two fugitives had not been in the house, Denis told them, and Jessie repeated what she suspected.

"Then we'll get the police boat after them. Come on!"

When Alley returned to the rooming house, Dutch had been up and waiting for him. "Where the hell you been?"

"What you all riled up for? Why ain't you in bed?"

"I couldn't sleep. The goddamn coppers is lookin' for us. You been out chasin' a girl?"

Alley grinned. "I caught one." Dutch was edgy as hell. When he got that way, he wanted to move around. Alley said,

166

"Come on, Dutch, we can head outa here in the morning."

"No. Let's get out now—tonight!"

Alley was tired. "Tonight? Jesus!"

"Get your duds together. We going to the levee." Dutch pulled a pistol, flicked open the loading gate and looked at the brass. Satisfied, he thrust it into his belt. He had a bag already packed. "Hurry up, get moving."

They slid out silently, locking the doors behind them. There was not a sound in the house. They moved along the misty street toward the river.

The levee was busy all round the clock. It was lighted by lanterns and sticks of wood burning in iron baskets. Dutch said, "If our luck is turnin' good, we'll find the *Scout*."

Their luck was excellent.

The small steamboat had arrived only hours earlier, and Captain Dorman was surprised to see them. "I thought you was in St. Louis."

"We come back. You take us upriver, Augie?"

"Yeah, but not until tomorra. I just got in. Got to unload and take on cargo in the morning." He looked them over. "You in a hurry?"

Dutch said, "We ain't too welcome here."

"Get in the cabin." Augie was watching the levee. "Stay outa sight so nobody wonders what you doing here." He gave them blankets and they curled up in a corner.

In the morning they ate hard bread and sausage. Augie had some of it in a cooler. They stayed inside while men unloaded the boat. A wagon showed up with barrels, and they were hauled on board and lashed down. Augie came into the cabin now and then to tell them to keep their heads down. "They's coppers on the levee."

In an hour he said, "We getting steam up. We'll be gone pretty soon."

The police boat was named *Hiram Gagnaire*, a trim craft, a stern-wheeler painted white with maroon touches. It was captained by a piratical-looking riverman, Lucas Jarnoux. He and Denis were obviously old friends; Jarnoux bowed over Jessica's hand like a diplomat.

"I am delighted to have you on board, Miss Starbuck."

"Thank you . . ."

Denis explained they were eager to overtake the *Scout*, to question the crew and possible passengers. They suspected that the notorious outlaw Dutch Rollins was aboard. Jarnoux smiled. He knew the boat, he said, and also knew Captain Dorman, who was a very slippery customer.

The *Scout* was possibly an hour ahead, but Jarnoux confidently expected he would overtake them before nightfall . . . barring unforeseen complications.

He said, "If Dorman is carrying Dutch, I can impound his boat. It will give me much pleasure to take that rascal off the river."

Jarnoux was captain and pilot and took the *Gagnaire* up the river skillfully, stopping only for wood. He paced the deck impatiently as the loading took place.

Five hours into the chase, when they stopped, a woodhawk told them the *Scout* was less than a half hour ahead.

The sky was gradually losing color, turning gray as clouds slid across the dying sun and the shadows deepened. With binoculars to his eyes, Captain Jarnoux said, "She's just ahead." He handed the glasses to Jessie.

The other steamboat was just disappearing around a bend as she looked. Jarnoux said, "She's only about two miles ahead now."

"What's our strategy?" Ki asked.

Jarnoux tapped his white teeth. "We'll come up close and tell him to stop for boarding. We have a two-pounder cannon to enforce our request." He pointed to the brass gun on the foredeck.

"He's seen us," Foucaud said. "There's more smoke . . ."

Jarnoux smiled. "He's probably burning everything that will go into his firebox, but he won't get away from us. This boat is faster than most."

They were drawing nearer. Then suddenly a rifle shot cracked over their heads. Jarnoux yelled for them to take cover. "They know we're a police boat. And now that they've fired on us, I can sink them."

168

They were around the bend, and the *Scout* was dead ahead in the straight river. Jarnoux gave quick orders, and crewmen ran to man the small cannon. Jessie watched them shove in the power bag, then a round ball. A man stooped to aim the piece while another moved it with a handspike as the gun captain directed. Then the man stood aside with a lanyard. When he jerked it the gun fired. Smoke spurted from the muzzle, and Jessie saw a big splash appear in front of the other boat.

"Just over," someone shouted.

"Fire another round," Jarnoux ordered.

But Captain Dorman had had enough. The *Scout* headed for the bank, coasting along in slack water. One single cannon ball could sink him or do great damage to his frail craft.

As the *Gagnaire* came close, Dorman backed his paddle wheels and the boat nudged the bank and stopped.

And instantly Dutch and Alley jumped to the shore and ran into the trees as Jessie and Ki yelled.

Jarnoux put his boat next to the *Scout*, and Jessie, Ki and Denis ran across to the bank. Ki led the way into the woods. It was dark, as night settled in. Ki went slowly, looking for movement. Would the two fugitives ambush them or go on as fast as possible to put distance between them? It was impossible to know.

Dutch and Alley were as dangerous as hungry tigers and were doubtless on edge, enough to shoot at anything.

They came to a high grassy bank. There were fresh marks showing the two had climbed it a very short time ago. Ki gazed up into the shadows. They might be waiting there . . .

Denis saw the situation at once. "I'll go one way; you go the other."

Ki nodded and they separated. He and Jessie went to the left a dozen yards and climbed the bank silently. It was perhaps twelve feet to the weedy top. When he reached it, Ki peered over, seeing no one.

The trees were thick and it was very dark. There was an exchange of shots far to their right. Ki saw the orange blossoms, and he gritted his teeth, hearing Jessie gasp. Had Denis run into both of them?

But suddenly someone came toward them, pushing through the brush. Ki went to his knees, motioning to Jessie, but she stood, yanking back the hammer of her pistol.

It was Dutch! He snapped a shot at her. The bullet rapped into a tree over Ki's head. He heard Dutch thumb back the hammer again, and he threw the *shuriken*.

Dutch was flung to one side. Ki rushed to him, but Dutch was dead, his throat torn out. Ki turned as Denis appeared and Jessie went to him. "Are you all right?"

"It is over," Denis said, glancing at Dutch's body. He had shot Alley Trask as Alley came toward him in the gloom. "He saw me too late."

Captain Jarnoux had his crewmen wrap the two bodies and haul them aboard. August Dorman was under arrest, and several crewmen manned his boat and followed the *Gagnaire* back to the New Orleans levee.

She wanted a bath and a good night's sleep, Jessica said. Then she wanted to go and see Aunt Lydia.

GILES TIPPETTE

Author of the best-selling WILSON YOUNG
SERIES, BAD NEWS, and CROSS FIRE

is back with his most exciting
Western adventure yet!

JAILBREAK

Time is running out for Justa Williams, owner of the Half-
Moon Ranch in West Texas. His brother Norris is being
held in a Mexican jail, and neither bribes nor threats can
free him.

Now, with the help of a dozen kill-crazy Mexican *banditos*,
Justa aims to blast Norris out. But the worst is yet to come:
a hundred-mile chase across the Mexican desert with fifty
federales in hot pursuit.

The odds of reaching the Texas border are a million to
nothing . . . and if the Williams brothers don't watch their
backs, the road to freedom could turn into the road to hell!

Turn the page for an exciting preview of

Jailbreak
by
Giles Tippette

On sale now, wherever Jove Books are sold!

At supper Norris, my middle brother, said, "I think we got some trouble on that five thousand acres down on the border near Laredo."

He said it serious, which is the way Norris generally says everything. I quit wrestling with the steak Buttercup, our cook, had turned into rawhide and said, "What are you talking about? How could we have trouble on land lying idle?"

He said, "I got word from town this afternoon that a telegram had come in from a friend of ours down there. He says we got some kind of squatters taking up residence on the place."

My youngest brother, Ben, put his fork down and said, incredulously, "*That* five thousand acres? Hell, it ain't nothing but rocks and cactus and sand. Why in hell would anyone want to squat on that worthless piece of nothing?"

Norris just shook his head. "I don't know. But that's what the telegram said. Came from Jack Cole. And if anyone ought to know what's going on down there it would be him."

I thought about it and it didn't make a bit of sense. I was Justa Williams, and my family, my two brothers and myself and our father, Howard, occupied a considerable ranch called the Half-Moon down along the Gulf of Mexico in Matagorda County, Texas. It was some of the best grazing land in the state and we had one of the best herds of purebred and crossbred cattle in that part of the country. In short we were pretty well-to-do.

But that didn't make us any the less ready to be stolen from, if indeed that was the case. The five thousand acres Norris had been talking about had come to us through a trade our father had made some years before. We'd never made any use of the land, mainly because, as Ben had said, it was pretty worthless and because it was a good two hundred miles from our ranch headquarters. On a few occasions we'd bought cattle in Mexico and then used the acreage to hold small groups on while we made up a herd. But other than that, it lay mainly forgotten.

I frowned. "Norris, this doesn't make a damn bit of sense. Right after supper send a man into Blessing with a return wire for Jack asking him if he's certain. What the hell kind of squatting could anybody be doing on that land?"

Ben said, "Maybe they're raisin' watermelons." He laughed.

I said, "They could raise melons, but there damn sure wouldn't be no water in them."

Norris said, "Well, it bears looking into." He got up, throwing his napkin on the table. "I'll go write out that telegram."

I watched him go, dressed, as always, in his town clothes. Norris was the businessman in the family. He'd been sent down to the University at Austin and had got considerable learning about the ins and outs of banking and land deals and all the other parts of our business that didn't directly involve the ranch. At the age of twenty-nine I'd been the boss of the operation a good deal longer than I cared to think about. It had been thrust upon me by our father when I wasn't much more than twenty. He'd said he'd wanted me to take over while he was still strong enough to help me out of my mistakes and I reckoned that was partly true. But it had just seemed that after our mother had died the life had sort of gone out of him. He'd been one of the earliest settlers, taking up the land not long after Texas had become a republic in 1845. I figured all the

176

years of fighting Indians and then Yankees and scalawags and carpetbaggers and cattle thieves had taken their toll on him. Then a few years back he'd been nicked in the lungs by a bullet that should never have been allowed to heed his way and it had thrown an extra strain on his heart. He was pushing seventy and he still had plenty of head on his shoulders, but mostly all he did now was sit around in his rocking chair and stare out over the cattle and land business he'd built. Not to say that I didn't go to him for advice when the occasion demanded. I did, and mostly I took it.

Buttercup came in just then and sat down at the end of the table with a cup of coffee. He was near as old as Dad and almost completely worthless. But he'd been one of the first hands that Dad had hired and he'd been kept on even after he couldn't sit a horse anymore. The problem was he'd elected himself cook, and that was the sorriest day our family had ever seen. There were two Mexican women hired to cook for the twelve riders we kept full time, but Buttercup insisted on cooking for the family.

Mainly, I think, because he thought he was one of the family. A notion we could never completely dissuade him from.

So he sat there, about two days of stubble on his face, looking as scrawny as a pecked-out rooster, sweat running down his face, his apron a mess. He said, wiping his forearm across his forehead, "Boy, it shore be hot in there. You boys shore better be glad you ain't got no business takes you in that kitchen."

Ben said, in a loud mutter, "I wish you didn't either."

Ben, at twenty-five, was easily the best man with a horse or a gun that I had ever seen. His only drawback was that he was hotheaded and he tended to act first and think later. That ain't a real good combination for someone that could go on the prod as fast as Ben. When I had argued with Dad about taking over as boss, suggesting instead that Norris, with his education, was a much better choice, Dad had simply said, "Yes, in some ways. But he can't handle Ben. You can. You can handle Norris, too. But none of them can handle you."

Well, that hadn't been exactly true. If Dad had wished it I would have taken orders from Norris even though he was two years younger than me. But the logic in Dad's line of thinking had been that the Half-Moon and our cattle business was the lodestone of all our businesses and only I could run that. He had been right. In the past I'd imported purebred Whiteface and Hereford cattle from up North, bred them to our native Longhorns and produced cattle that would bring twice as much at market as the horse-killing, all-bone, all-wild Longhorns. My neighbors had laughed at me at first, claiming those square little purebreds would never make it in our Texas heat. But they'd been wrong and, one by one, they'd followed the example of the Half-Moon.

Buttercup was setting up to take off on another one of his long-winded harangues about how it had been in the "old days" so I quickly got up, excusing myself, and went into the big office we used for sitting around in as well as a place of business. Norris was at the desk composing his telegram so I poured myself out a whiskey and sat down. I didn't want to hear about any trouble over some worthless five thousand acres of borderland. In fact I didn't want to hear about any troubles of any kind. I was just two weeks short of getting married, married to a lady I'd been courting off and on for five years, and I was mighty anxious that nothing come up to interfere with our plans. Her name was Nora Parker and her daddy owned and run the general mercantile in our nearest town, Blessing. I'd almost lost her once before to a Kansas City drummer. She'd finally gotten tired of waiting on me, waiting until the ranch didn't occupy all my time, and almost run off with a smooth- talking Kansas City drummer that called on her daddy in the harness trade. But she'd come to her senses in time and got off the train in Texarkana and returned home.

But even then it had been a close thing. I, along with my men and brothers and help from some of our neighbors, had been involved with stopping a huge herd of illegal cattle being driven up from Mexico from crossing our range and infecting our cattle with tick fever which could have wiped us all out. I tell you it had been a bloody business. We'd lost four good men and had to kill at least a half dozen on the other side. Fact of the business was I'd come about as close as I ever had to getting killed myself, and

178

that was going some for the sort of rough-and-tumble life I'd led.

Nora had almost quit me over it; saying she just couldn't take the uncertainty. But in the end, she'd stuck by me. That had been the year before, 1896, and I'd convinced her that civilized law was coming to the country, but until it did, we that had been there before might have to take things into our own hands from time to time.

She'd seen that and had understood. I loved her and she loved me and that was enough to overcome any of the trouble we were still likely to encounter from day to day.

So I was giving Norris a pretty sour look as he finished his telegram and sent for a hired hand to ride it into Blessing, seven miles away. I said, "Norris, let's don't make a big fuss about this. That land ain't even crossed my mind in at least a couple of years. Likely we got a few Mexican families squatting down there and trying to scratch out a few acres of corn."

Norris gave me his businessman's look. He said, "It's our land, Justa. And if we allow anyone to squat on it for long enough or put up a fence they can lay claim. That's the law. My job is to see that we protect what we have, not give it away."

I sipped at my whiskey and studied Norris. In his town clothes he didn't look very impressive. He'd inherited more from our mother than from Dad so he was not as wide-shouldered and slim-hipped as Ben and me. But I knew him to be a good, strong, dependable man in any kind of fight. Of course he wasn't that good with a gun, but then Ben I weren't all that good with books like he was. But I said, just to jolly him a bit, "Norris, I do believe you are running to suet. I may have to put you out with Ben working the horse herd and work a little of that fat off you."

Naturally it got his goat. Norris had always envied Ben and me a little. I was just over six foot and weighed right around a hundred and ninety. I had inherited my daddy's big hands and big shoulders. Ben was almost a copy of me except he was about a size smaller. Norris said, "I weigh the same as I have for the last five years. If it's any of your business."

179

I said, as if I was being serious, "Must be them sack suits you wear. What they do, pad them around the middle?"

He said, "Why don't you just go to hell."

After he'd stomped out of the room I got the bottle of whiskey and an extra glass and went down to Dad's room. It had been one of his bad days and he'd taken to bed right after lunch. Strictly speaking he wasn't supposed to have no whiskey, but I watered him down a shot every now and then and it didn't seem to do him no harm.

He was sitting up when I came in the room. I took a moment to fix him a little drink, using some water out of his pitcher, then handed him the glass and sat down in the easy chair by the bed. I told him what Norris had reported and asked what he thought.

He took a sip of his drink and shook his head. "Beats all I ever heard," he said. "I took that land in trade for a bad debt some fifteen, twenty years ago. I reckon I'd of been money ahead if I'd of hung on to the bad debt. That land won't even raise weeds, well as I remember, and Noah was in on the last rain that fell on the place."

We had considerable amounts of land spotted around the state as a result of this kind of trade or that. It was Norris's business to keep up with their management. I was just bringing this to Dad's attention more out of boredom and impatience for my wedding day to arrive than anything else.

I said, "Well, it's a mystery to me. How you feeling?"

He half smiled. "Old." Then he looked into his glass. "And I never liked watered whiskey. Pour me a dollop of the straight stuff in here."

I said, "Now, Howard. You know—"

He cut me off. "If I wanted somebody to argue with I'd send for Buttercup. Now do like I told you."

I did, but I felt guilty about it. He took the slug of whiskey down in one pull. Then he leaned his head back on the pillow and said, "Aaaaah. I don't give a damn what that horse doctor says, ain't nothing makes a man feel as good inside as a shot of the best."

I felt sorry for him laying there. He'd always led just the kind of life he wanted—going where he wanted, doing what

180

he wanted, having what he set out to get. And now he was reduced to being a semi-invalid. But one thing that showed the strength that was still in him was that you *never* heard him complain. He said, "How's the cattle?"

I said, "They're doing all right, but I tell you we could do with a little of Noah's flood right now. All this heat and no rain is curing the grass off way ahead of time. If it doesn't let up we'll be feeding hay by late September, early October. And that will play hell on our supply. Could be we won't have enough to last through the winter. Norris thinks we ought to sell of five hundred herd or so, but the market is doing poorly right now. I'd rather chance the weather than take a sure beating by selling off."

He sort of shrugged and closed his eyes. The whiskey was relaxing him. He said, "You're the boss."

"Yeah," I said. "Damn my luck."

I wandered out of the back of the house. Even though it was nearing seven o'clock of the evening it was still good and hot. Off in the distance, about a half a mile away, I could see the outline of the house I was building for Nora and myself. It was going to be a close thing to get it finished by our wedding day. Not having any riders to spare for the project, I'd imported a a building contractor from Galveston, sixty miles away. He'd arrived with a half a dozen Mexican laborers and a few skilled masons and they'd set up a little tent city around the place. The contractor had gone back to Galveston to fetch some materials, leaving his Mexicans behind. I walked along idly, hoping he wouldn't forget that the job wasn't done. He had some of my money, but not near what he'd get when he finished the job.

Just then Ray Hays came hurrying across the back lot toward me. Ray was kind of a special case for me. The only problem with that was that he knew it and wasn't a bit above taking advantage of the situation. Once, a few years past, he'd saved my life by going against an evil man that he was working for at the time, an evil man who meant to have my life. In gratitude I'd given Ray a good job at the Half-Moon, letting him work directly under Ben, who was responsible for the horse herd. He was a good, steady man and a good man with a gun. He was also fair company. When he wasn't talking.

He came churning up to me, mopping his brow. He said, "Lordy, boss, it is—"

I said, "Hays, if you say it's hot I'm going to knock you down."

He gave me a look that was a mixture of astonishment and hurt. He said, "Why, whatever for?"

I said, "*Everybody* knows it's hot. Does every son of a bitch you run into have to make mention of the fact?"

His brow furrowed. "Well, I never thought of it that way. I 'spect you are right. Goin' down to look at yore house?"

I shook my head. "No. It makes me nervous to see how far they've got to go. I can't see any way it'll be ready on time."

He said, "Miss Nora ain't gonna like that."

I gave him a look. "I guess you felt forced to say that."

He looked down. "Well, maybe she won't mind."

I said, grimly, "The hell she won't. She'll think I did it a-purpose."

"Aw, she wouldn't."

"Naturally you know so much about it, Hays. Why don't you tell me a few other things about her."

"I was just tryin' to lift yore spirits, boss."

I said, "You keep trying to lift my spirits and I'll put you on the haying crew."

He looked horrified. No real cowhand wanted any work he couldn't do from the back of his horse. Haying was a hot, hard, sweaty job done either afoot or from a wagon seat. We generally brought in contract Mexican labor to handle ours. But I'd been known in the past to discipline a cowhand by giving him a few days on the hay gang. Hays said, "Boss, now I never meant nothin'. I swear. You know me, my mouth gets to runnin' sometimes. I swear I'm gonna watch it."

I smiled. Hays always made me smile. He was so easily buffaloed. He had it soft at the Half-Moon and he knew it and didn't want to take any chances on losing a good thing.

I lit up a cigarillo and watched dusk settle in over the coastal plains. It wasn't but three miles to Matagorda Bay and it was quiet enough I felt like I could almost hear the waves breaking on the shore. Somewhere in the distance a mama cow bawled for her calf. The spring crop were near about weaned by now, but there were still a few mamas that wouldn't cut the apron strings. I stood there reflecting on how peaceful things had been of late. It suited me just fine. All I wanted was to get my house finished, marry Nora and never handle another gun so long as I lived.

The peace and quiet were short-lived. Within twenty-four hours we'd had a return telegram from Jack Cole. It said:

YOUR LAND OCCUPIED BY TEN TO TWELVE MEN STOP CAN'T BE SURE WHAT THEY'RE DOING BECAUSE THEY RUN STRANGERS OFF STOP APPEAR TO HAVE A GOOD MANY CATTLE GATHERED STOP APPEAR TO BE FENCING STOP ALL I KNOW STOP

I read the telegram twice and then I said, "Why this is crazy as hell! That land wouldn't support fifty head of cattle."

We were all gathered in the big office. Even Dad was there, sitting in his rocking chair. I looked up at him. "What do you make of this, Howard?"

He shook his big, old head of white hair. "Beats the hell out of me, Justa. I can't figure it."

Ben said, "Well, I don't see where it has to be figured. I'll take five men and go down there and run them off. I don't care what they're doing. They ain't got no business on our land."

I said, "Take it easy, Ben. Aside from the fact you don't need to be getting into any more fights this year, I can't spare you or five men. The way this grass is drying up we've got to keep drifting those cattle."

Norris said, "No, Ben is right. We can't have such affairs going on with our property. But we'll handle it within the law. I'll simply take the train down there, hire a good lawyer and have the matter settled by the sheriff. Shouldn't take but a few days."

Well, there wasn't much I could say to that. We couldn't very well let people take advantage of us, but I still hated to be without Norris's services even for a few days. On matters other than the ranch he was the expert, and it didn't seem like there was a day went by that some financial question didn't come up that only he could answer. I said, "Are you sure you can spare yourself for a few days?"

He thought for a moment and then nodded. "I don't see why not. I've just moved most of our available cash into short-term municipal bonds in Galveston. The market is looking all right and everything appears fine at the bank. I can't think of anything that might come up."

I said, "All right. But you just keep this in mind. You are not a gun hand. You are not a fighter. I do not want you going anywhere near those people, whoever they are. You do it legal and let the sheriff handle the eviction. Is that understood?"

He kind of swelled up, resenting the implication that he couldn't handle himself. The biggest trouble I'd had through the years when trouble had come up had been keeping Norris out of it. Why he couldn't just be content to be a wagon load of brains was more than I could understand. He said, "Didn't you just hear me say I intended to go through a lawyer and the sheriff? Didn't I just say that?"

I said, "I wanted to be sure you heard yourself."

He said, "Nothing wrong with my hearing. Nor my approach to this matter. You seem to constantly be taken with the idea that I'm always looking for a fight. I think you've got the wrong brother. I use logic."

"Yeah?" I said. "You remember when that guy kicked you in the balls when they were holding guns on us? And then we chased them twenty miles and finally caught them?"

He looked away. "That has nothing to do with this."

"Yeah?" I said, enjoying myself. "And here's this guy, shot all to hell. And what was it you insisted on doing?"

Ben laughed, but Norris wouldn't say anything.

I said, "Didn't you insist on us standing him up so you could kick him in the balls? Didn't you?"

He sort of growled, "Oh, go to hell."

I said, "I just want to know where the logic was in that."

He said, "Right is right. I was simply paying him back in kind. It was the only thing his kind could understand."

I said, "That's my point. You just don't go down there and go to paying back a bunch of rough hombres in kind. Or any other currency for that matter."

184

That made him look over at Dad. He said, "Dad, will you make him quit treating me like I was ten years old? He does it on purpose."

But he'd appealed to the wrong man. Dad just threw his hands in the air and said, "Don't come to me with your troubles. I'm just a boarder around here. You get your orders from Justa. You know that."

Of course he didn't like that. Norris had always been a strong hand for the right and wrong of a matter. In fact, he may have been one of the most stubborn men I'd ever met. But he didn't say anything, just gave me a look and muttered something about hoping a mess came up at the bank while he was gone and then see how much boss I was.

But he didn't mean nothing by it. Like most families, we fought amongst ourselves and, like most families, God help the outsider who tried to interfere with one of us.

A special offer for people who enjoy reading the best Westerns published today. If you enjoyed this book, subscribe now and get . . .

TWO FREE

A $5.90 VALUE—NO OBLIGATION

If you enjoyed this book and would like to read more of the very best Westerns being published today, you'll want to subscribe to True Value's Western Home Subscription Service. If you enjoyed the book you just read and want more of the most exciting, adventurous, action packed Westerns, subscribe now.

Each month the editors of True Value will select the 6 very best Westerns from America's leading publishers for special readers like you. You'll be able to preview these new titles as soon as they are published, FREE for ten days with no obligation.

TWO FREE BOOKS

When you subscribe, we'll send you your first month's shipment of the newest and best 6 Westerns for you to preview. With your first shipment, two of these books will be yours as our introductory gift to you absolutely FREE, regardless of what you decide to do. If you like them, as much as we think you will, keep all six books but pay for just 4 at the low subscriber rate of just $2.45 each. If you decide to return them, keep 2 of the titles as our gift. No obligation.

Special Subscriber Savings

When you become a True Value subscriber you'll save money several ways. First, all regular monthly selections will be billed at the low subscriber price of just $2.45 each. That's

WESTERNS!

at least a savings of $3.00 each month below the publishers price. Second, there is never any shipping, handling or other hidden charges—Free home delivery. What's more there is no minimum number of books you must buy, you may return any selection for full credit and you can cancel your subscription at any time. A TRUE VALUE!

Mail the coupon below

To start your subscription and receive 2 FREE WESTERNS, fill out the coupon below and mail it today. We'll send your first shipment which includes 2 FREE BOOKS as soon as we receive it.

Mail To:
True Value Home Subscription Services, Inc.   10614
P.O. Box 5235
120 Brighton Road
Clifton, New Jersey 07015-5235

YES! I want to start receiving the very best Westerns being published today. Send me my first shipment of 6 Westerns for me to preview FREE for 10 days. If I decide to keep them, I'll pay for just 4 of the books at the low subscriber price of $2.45 each; a total of $9.80 (a $17.70 value). Then each month I'll receive the 6 newest and best Westerns to preview Free for 10 days. If I'm not satisfied I may return them within 10 days and owe nothing. Otherwise I'll be billed at the special low subscriber rate of $2.45 each; a total of $14.70 (at least a $17.70 value) and save $3.00 off the publishers price. There are never any shipping, handling or other hidden charges. I understand I am under no obligation to purchase any number of books and I can cancel my subscription at any time, no questions asked. In any case the 2 FREE books are mine to keep.

Name _____

Address _____ Apt. # _____

City _____ State _____ Zip _____

Telephone # _____

Signature _____
                    (if under 18 parent or guardian must sign)
                    Terms and prices subject to change.
        Orders subject to acceptance by True Value Home Subscription Services, Inc.